To Brian

A cure for insomnia.

Best wishes
Ken Knight

Rambling Rhymes

About the Author

Kev Reynolds is a travel writer with more than fifty books to his name. Most of these are published by Cicerone Press (www.cicerone.co.uk) and devoted to mountain and countryside regions as far apart as Southern England and the high Himalaya. He has also published two volumes of memoir: A Walk in the Clouds and Abode of the Gods. The first of these is a collection of 75 short stories gathered from fifty years of mountain adventure; the second describes eight of his trekking expeditions in Nepal. This is his first book of verse – many of the subjects of these rhymes are based on people he's met and places explored during his travels. He lives in rural contentment in the Kentish countryside. (www.kevreynolds.co.uk)

Rambling Rhymes

by
Kev Reynolds

© Kev Reynolds 2020
© Clare Crooke (Cover illustration)

All rights reserved. No part of this publication may be reproduced or transmitted in any form or by any means without prior written permission of the copyright holder.

Privately published by the author at www.kevreynolds.co.uk

Acknowledgements

My thanks to Françoise Besson and Ian Maple for their insistence that I should publish these poems in a book, and to Clare Crooke and Siân Pritchard-Jones for making it possible. And, of course, special thanks to my wife for getting us both through Lockdown with love and laughter.

Contents

	Introduction	7
1	Twelve weeks	9
2	A prison without bars	11
3	The face at the window	13
4	Space between	15
5	Between here and there	17
6	Confused? You bet	19
7	The wanderer	21
8	It's better here than there and back	25
9	You should have seen me then	28
10	Why so glum, Chum?	30
11	Nature close to home	33
12	The cage	35
13	A turn around the garden	37
14	One foot in front of the other	40
15	In a spin	41
16	The didgeridoo	43
17	An owl around midnight	47
18	The surprise of the familiar	49
19	The call	52
20	Not silence, but peace	54
21	The quest	56
22	The traveller	57
23	Where the wild winds blow	59
24	Above the clouds	61
25	Six years	65

26	A friend indeed	69
27	Heaven's door	72
28	Three in one	74
29	Blame global warming	79
30	A cavern of ice	81
31	My friend Fred	84
32	The painted mountains	89
33	Living on air	91
34	Shrinking horizons	98
35	Back to the mountains	101
36	Along the Pyrenees	103
37	An end and a beginning	106
38	The lost mountain	109
39	The enchanted mountains	112
40	Adagio without strings	115
41	The memory box	118
42	Sleeping around	122
43	Helga	126
44	The old man of the mountains	129
45	Sacred ground	133
46	Kangchenjunga dreaming	136
47	Journey to Ladakh	139
48	A time and a place to remember	145
49	In the saddle	151
50	The hidden land	158

Introduction

In 1972 I had a poem published in The Countryman magazine; it was a piece of blank verse for which I was paid £1. Reading it again now I consider the editor was being rather generous.

I made no further attempt to write poetry, and in 1986 became a travel writer specialising in mountains and the countryside, rambling among some of the most dramatic places on Earth. I still consider it the World's Best Job.

Then came the Covid-19 pandemic. There was almost universal lockdown and in the spring of 2020 commissions for travel books dried up. But I'm lucky, I live in a beautiful part of the country, and even if it was out of bounds for a while, I knew that as soon as lockdown was lifted, I'd be able to get out there to enjoy it. Out There is where I belong

Suddenly, without any prodding, a poem appeared. The following day, another, then another. I have no idea where they came from, nor what sparked them, but with more than a hundred having now been produced, and in response to many requests from friends and neighbours, I've gathered a selection for this little book. I make no claim for their quality as 'poetry' – they are little more than rhyming verse;

some consist of a few stanzas of nonsense, while others are longer tales – stories (ballads) told in verse. I am, after all, a story-teller, and while a number of these ballads take place among mountains far away, I hope you will gain as much enjoyment from reading them as I did putting them down on paper.

Kev Reynolds
Kent

1: Twelve weeks

Twelve weeks of isolation? That's got to be a jest
If so, it's not a funny one, its outcome I detest.
My nose pressed to the window, I need to go outside,
Out there in the sunshine, watching buzzards glide.
They glide in graceful circles, often there are two
Adding something special to my favourite hilltop view.

Instead I'm all alone in here, alone with just my thoughts,
Plus a bag of groceries a kindly neighbour brought.
Old, frail and vulnerable – is that really me?
What happened to those glory years when I would wander free?
Free, oh yes the world was mine, I'd travel where I chose
Now it's lonely isolation, with doors and windows closed

Pull yourself together man, stop whingeing like a fool!
You know you're not alone in this, we're all in one great pool.
Instead of giving in to useless moments of self-pity,
Just thank your lucky stars that you're not living in a city.
Here at least you've got some flowers, a lawn of green green grass,
A glimpse of Nature's goodness just beyond the glass.

Between the other houses I can see a line of hills
A thousand times I've walked up there, a cure for all my ills.
Now should I be downhearted, or when I'm feeling low
I'll close my eyes and in my thoughts that's just where I will go.
Imagination is a gift, and so is memory,
Put the two together and I'm as happy as can be.

When I was young and innocent with no plan for tomorrow,
I'd take each day that came along and care not what would follow.
With my passport and a rucksack I sought out distant lands,
I roamed the world, I sailed the seas and slept on golden sands.
In steamy jungles far away among exotic trees
I dropped each daily highlight in the well of memories.

With twelve weeks' isolation I can look into that well
And gather up adventures, all those stories I could tell!
They don't need much embellishment, they're better with the truth,
And despite the years I still recall the innocence of youth.
So I will go where once I went when young and fancy free
Then twelve weeks of isolation will hardly bother me.

2: A prison without bars

Lockdown's not a sentence in a prison without bars,
we can go into the garden and dance among the stars.
No shackles round our ankles, no chains to hold us down,
no armed police at checkpoints on the edge of every town.

Were padlocks locking my front door they'd still not keep me home,
a view 'out there' is all I need to set me free to roam.
Let politicians make the rules I'll do my best to keep,
Though drifting in my mind's eye with the restlessness of sheep.

I need not go outside the house beyond my garden gate
I'm free to get up early or stay in bed 'til late,
While in my head a thousand faces come to say 'how do' -
Friends in foreign places, in lockdown just like you.

Do they complain? Not in my dreams, they're as they were of old
In days we went adventuring, pretending we were bold,
I hear their voices loud and clear, I hear their laughter too,
And there's no doubt that they all know precisely what to do.

Like you and me they have a well, a well that won't run dry,
It's full of happy memories we share both you and I,
The simple things that brought such joy, like walks through summer fields
When we'd feast on all the bounty that Mother Nature yields.

I think of mountains that we climbed I'll never see again -
Though truth be told they're still in reach along my memory lane
Where time stands still, the old are young, and it never ever rains
And anything is possible; it's all wins and all gains.

Now dip your bucket in that well and gently draw it up,
Then sip a favourite memory for which you'll need no cup.
Days of old are vintage days when drunk a second time,
So close your eyes, and settle down to sip sweet mem'ry's wine.

No! Lockdown's not a sentence in a prison without bars,
Use your imagination to dance among the stars
And from that well of memory you can slake your thirst
To see how young you can become despite the lockdown curse.

3: The face at the window

There's a face up at the window of number forty-two
Gazing into space, perhaps remembering a view,
A view or maybe just a dream of somewhere far away
Somewhere out of bounds until there'll dawn a brighter day.

There's a light up at the window of number forty-two,
It makes me wonder if perhaps there's something I should do.
Could it be a call for help from strangers passing by,
Or just a lonely fella who can only see the sky?

It's there all day that yellow light at number forty-two,
It's on all night and just as bright at one o'clock or two.
The face is at the window, no curtains blocking light,
A face with hollow empty eyes, could they be lacking sight?

That face it never seems to leave the light at forty-two,
The only time it moves is when I adjust my view,
But I know that moments later it will be there just the same -
A face up at the window, a face without a name.

One day I crossed the street and knocked at number forty-two.
At last an old man answered and said: 'Ah! So it is you.
I've waited days and weeks to see if you would say hello
I'd have crossed the street to visit you but I am very slow.'

'Are you okay?' I asked the man at number forty-two,
'I'm living all alone,' he said, 'with nothing much to do

I find these days so dull to live in endless isolation
The only way to deal with it is quiet meditation.'

He showed me to the garden at number forty-two.
'I'll make a cuppa if you like, with biscuits just for you.
I'd like to hear about your life and what you do all day
The books you read, the food you eat, the music that you play.'

I liked this lonely fella at number forty-two,
He told me that he loved the sunshine and the morning dew.
We had so much in common I found to my surprise,
That all of life's adventures were written in his eyes.

The eyes that graced the window at number forty-two,
Responded with affection as our new-found friendship grew.
The light was no more needed for he knew that I'd be there,
At last he'd found a neighbour who would really, truly care.

4: Space between

When man looked down to earth from space
he saw an amazing sight,
half the world was full of day,
the other, black with night.
He sat there in his man-made box,
an astronaut alone,
what were his inner thoughts, d'you think
as he spun so far from home?

The prospect fills me with real dread,
my heart beats wild with fear.
I'd never turn my back upon
so much that I hold dear.
For life on earth is rich and good,
or it is for lots of us,
though not for many others
too poor to make a fuss.

That double-sided planet
displayed from outer space
tells us all we need to know
about the human race.
Life isn't what it ought to be,
we haven't learned to share,
we turn our backs on those without
for whom we ought to care.
We who bask in sunshine

make sure we're at the top,
and race towards tomorrow's gold
and seldom pause – or stop
to think of those we tread upon
to fulfil our dearest dreams,
while they stumble in the darkness -
or that is how it seems.

That view of earth from outer space
is one we're used to now.
We often see it on tv
whose newscasts show us how
there's famine here, war raging there,
our minds then drift away.
All woes are simply pushed aside
until another day.

The light side and the dark side,
both viewed by man from space
ought shake us from our lethargy
to reflect upon the grace
and the life we take for granted
while others just survive.
If we learned to share the gifts we have
all humanity could thrive.

5: Between here and there

It's like a moat round a castle
that has yet to be bridged,
it's the big strawberry jelly
taken out of the fridge.
It's the hush that precedes
each September dawn,
or the cry that you wait for
when a baby's been born.

It's the intake of breath
when you jump in the sea;
it's that hinge Nature's made
at the back of your knee.
It's not part of laughter
nor is it a sigh,
it's the first thing you notice
when you focus your eye.

It's too large for a rabbit
too small for a hare,
too much for one portion,
insufficient to share.
It breaks through the darkness
with a big beam of light,
a bit like a comet
on a still summer's night.

It defies definition,
it has no real name,
it's almost like this –
but not quite the same.
You reach out to touch it
then find that it's gone.
Now that can't be right -
but nor is it wrong.

Forgive my confusion,
I'm not always this bad,
should I ignore it
or remain feeling sad?
For once in my life
I should know what to say
before that grey fog
takes the right words away.

So I stand all alone
in a room full of friends,
amid all the silence
their laughter transcends.
It's then that I realise
there's no need to despair
for I've discovered I'm caught
between here and there.

*

6: Confused? You bet

It can't be easy speaking English when you're fresh upon these shores,
At times our language doesn't make much sense.
Give your answer yes or no
And don't sit on the fence.

If you want to be a friend to all, make your intentions clear
Don't dilly-dally, go ahead, be bold.
Don't change your mood from day to day,
Please don't blow hot and cold.

A friend in need's a friend indeed, that's something we believe
Stay faithful, straight and true
For should you let them badly down
You'll find the air turns blue.

Your date might be a dolly bird,
Your mate a Jack-the-Lad,
While an elderly gent's another old bloke
Who happens to be someone's dad.

That pet you take out on a lead
Is a dog, a pooch or a hound,
But if you should meet an aggressive one
You really must stand your ground.

Don't harbour any resentment,
Just assume what will be will be,

Keep your friendships on an even keel
And remain as fit as a flea.

An apple a day keeps the doctor away,
But never a plum or a pear,
While the mop that's growing upon your bonce
Is neither a rabbit nor hare.

After lunch I could do with a toes-up,
Forty winks, a kip or a doss,
But my wife's a workaholic
And what's more she is the boss.

When you go upstairs and climb into bed,
I trust that you'll sleep like a log,
Then wake up as fresh as a daisy
And not feel sick as a dog.

Confused? Of course, you bet I am
And I've lived here all my life,
So have pity on the stranger
Who arrives with his trouble and strife.

Oh don't get me started with rhyming slang
It's like a Cockney disease.
Our language is bad enough as it is
Shall we leave it at that?
Don't tease!

7: The wanderer

Tall, he was, tall and dark
with long and unkempt hair,
his eyebrows stiff as yard brooms
above a long-lost stare.
His skin was tanned and wrinkled,
or perhaps it needed soap.
Yet something in his manner
spoke of real unbridled hope.

A rucksack settled on his back
containing all his wares,
and despite his lack of money
it seemed he had few cares;
a man content with how things were
and not how they might be,
he stepped across our empty street
just to talk to me.

'G'day,' he said with Ozzie twang,
'Mind if we have a chat?
I've hardly spoke with anyone
except a passing cat!
I've heard no news for many months,
most times that would be fine,
but people treat me different now
as if I'm guilty of a crime.'

'If someone sees me coming
they'll turn their heads away.
Or if there's time they'll cross the road
with no thought of delay.
Do I look so odd to you,
I'm an ordinary bloke
who likes to sit and spin a yarn
and share a silly joke.'

'I guess it's social distancing,
that's what it seems to be.
In fact you're just a bit too close -
please move six feet from me.'
'Six feet? Do I smell bad as that?
Forgive me if I do,
my last bath was on Christmas Day,
then I had another two.'

'No, no,' I said, 'it isn't that,
think lockdown for a start,
since caught in this pandemic
we have to keep apart.'
'Pandemic? What pandemic?
What's that all about?'
I stared then misbelieving –
did he try to catch me out?

'Now mister please don't play the fool,
the whole world's been brought low.

So we need to keep alert to risk -
that's something all should know.
How is it that you're ignorant,
have you spent six months asleep?'
'Not so,' the stranger told me,
'I roam the world on my two feet.'

'I sleep in lonely woodlands
in a weathered one-man tent,
and roam by day the byeways
that now take me right through Kent.
There's nothing much I want in towns,
Mother Nature fills my need,
and I have no care for papers
while I've books and maps to read.'

Oh Lord, I thought, he can't go on
but what will happen next?
Two weeks of isolation
will surely have him vexed.
'I'll tell you what, I've no spare bed
but a garden for your tent.
You can pitch it on our tiny lawn –
we'll not charge you any rent.'

So if you peer across our fence
and see a stranger there,
you'll know he's our lost wanderer,
the one with unkempt hair.

What happens when this fortnight's done
I simply have no clue,
should he resume his wandering?
What d'you think he should do?

8: It's better here, than there and back

The brightest brains in Britain get up before the lark
and leave their family sleeping as they creep off in the dark.
They drive off to the station where they park their fancy car,
by then the day is dawning to show them where they are.

They stand upon the platform in the same place every day
among the silent strangers who have nothing much to say.
It's far too soon to crank the brain or have some useful thought
so they peer into their smartphones or Daily Telegraph they bought.

The train is not quite full yet, there's still somewhere to sit
but others waiting down the line must see if they can fit.
If not they'll squeeze along the aisles, still dozing where they stand
for which they've paid a fortune for the tickets in their hand.

Once off the train in London, there's the jolly Underground
where every other worker it seems is also bound.
The carriages are airless, every one packed tight
and down there on the Circle Line it's neither day nor night.

At last they reach the office and sit down at their desk
where exhaustion from their journey has them yearning for a rest.
All day the phones are ringing, computer screens are everywhere
no natural light intrudes of course, and no hint of fresh air.

It's dark when work is over, daylight came and went
as they make their homeward journey, all energy now spent.
Their partner's waiting patiently, the kids tucked up in bed,
the days and weeks go by like this, and little has been said.

Should they think about it, they'd know that this is mad.
What about their families, the life they wished they'd had?
There's something not quite right here, it's like a crazy dream,
each life is worth much more than this, if you see what I mean.

But when we came to lockdown, most people stayed at home,
working on their laptops, backed up by telephone.
No need to get up early, they ate breakfast with the kids,
learning all about them, what their dreams were, what they did.

The spare room was the office, with its view of birds and trees,
and work was much less stressful, it was timed just as they please.
They could have a restful cuppa sitting outside in the sun
and discover work-life balance allowed some time for fun.

The brightest brains in Britain now enjoy the homes they bought,
with no need to go to London where life could be so fraught,
no need to spend a fortune while travelling so far,
so they call the local dealer and sell the second car.

I'm something of a country lad, the city's not for me,
I'd rather earn a pittance as long as I'm still free.
It's just as well that I was born without a working brain
or I'd be like all the clever ones who cursed the morning train.

So here we are, the lesson's learned, there's little more to say,
it's better here than there and back, commuting every day.
It's better for the family, you'll see the kids much more,
and a better work-life balance will be had, you can be sure.

9: You should have seen me then

My eyes have lost their sparkle, their focus mostly blurred,
my hips and knees are creaking, I know that sounds absurd.
I peer into the mirror and am shocked at what I see,
can that craggy-looking geezer in reality be me?

Last week I was a young man, the world was at my feet,
I'd swagger with a girl in tow – she lived just down the street.
Yes, I was young and dapper then, the best-dressed guy for miles,
I knew I turned the young girls' heads and loved their hungry smiles.

Sometimes I'd light a cigarette and lean against a wall,
I'd seen a film star do the same and thought it looked real cool.
My clothes were always chosen to match the latest style
but the way that fashion changes I'd only wear them for a while.

At discos and at dances I'd swing the girls around,
and knew each single guitar band, simply by their sound.
I'd crank the amplifiers up as loud as they would go,
that's why I'm hard of hearing now, too late for me I know.

I guess the days when I was young are catching up with me.
I'm old and deaf, I've lost my teeth, no longer fancy free.
My navel's heading southward, and I wobble when I walk,
and my wife's eyes lift up to heaven when I begin to talk.

Okay, I know, I can't complain, life's been a lot of fun,
but when I think about it, when all is said and done
I should have known much better in those days of way back when,
yet truth be told, I may be old, but I'd do it all again.

10: Why so glum, Chum?

He stumbles by, hood pulled up,
face focused on the ground.
His hands stuffed in his pockets,
earplugs thumping out their sound.

His shoulders hunched where ears should be,
you'd think he'd caught a chill,
his eyes are glazed, his flesh is white,
I wonder if he's ill.

He can't be more than seventeen,
has he lost the will to live?
He hasn't lived his life as yet,
there's so much that he can give.

What anxious thoughts go through his mind,
with what trouble's he beset?
It's as though he has a burden
that he simply can't forget.

I want to raise his eyes up
to see the world out there,
and to recognise its wonders,
as the wind blows through his hair.

It's time he heard the songs of dawn,
the chorus of each day,

he ought to feel the summer sun
and smell the dew-damp hay.

He should revel in the starlight,
sing praises to the moon,
and hang on to his innocence
for prudence comes too soon.

The precious years of childhood,
the days of youthful pride
are enriched by health and fitness
no young one should deride.

Don't waste them feeling angry,
nor let troubles weigh you down,
put a smile upon your fresh young face
and lose that old folks' frown.

Use the hours as best you can
and celebrate each day,
don't hanker for tomorrow
or long for yesterday.

You'll be old before you know it
if you waste these precious years,
so fill your life with laughter
and turn your back on fears.

For no-one loves a misery guts
who does nothing else but moan,
while there'll always be a welcome
for those whose sunshine fills their home.

So throw away your hoodie
and that gizmo belching sound,
wear the biggest smile you can
and be the richest guy around.

11: Nature close to home

The pandemic certainly taught me
the beauty of clouds in the sky,
The sun that comes up every morning,
The rivers that never run dry.

The mountains and deserts and oceans,
all creatures under the sun,
The insects and reptiles and all kinds of fish,
Without which our life comes undone.

It taught me that all of creation
evolves around Nature's fine laws,
An intricate web we've ignored til now
Revealing what damage we've caused.

Ignoring this truth all our lifetime
has satisfied none of our needs
And now we are feeling the backlash,
Paying for all our misdeeds.

Before this pandemic arrived here,
we held so much in disdain,
But now we can see life more clearly,
We'll take nothing for granted again.

The one thing it ought to have shown us,
is to treasure each day that arrives,

To value the Earth that sustains us,
Mistreat it, we'll never survive.

So stop what you're up to this moment,
there's something I'd like you to do
Take a deep breath in the garden
And accept that we're Nature too.

12: The cage

If it wasn't the birds it was muntjac deer,
if it wasn't the deer it was slugs,
if it wasn't for them or the butterfly's eggs
it would be a rich assortment of bugs.

There's black fly on the broad beans,
the leeks have turned yellow with rust,
the lettuces are going to seed too soon
and the courgettes have developed a crust.

Our neighbour's weeds and abundant seeds
drift across to our plot,
while the mice found their way to the strawberry bed
and ate the blessed lot.

The worst of the pests is a squirrel
who studies our fruit from a tree
and the moment we turn our backs on him
he thinks the pears are for him and they're free.

So I said to the man at the nursery,
'I could do with a cage for my wife'
and he looked at me through his glasses
and asked: 'for a short term or all of her life?'

'Oh no, you've got it all wrong,' I said,
'it's not to keep her shut in

but to keep the tiresome squirrels out
now surely that's not a sin?'

'I'll sell you the largest I have in stock'
he said with a look of glee,
'and since you tell me it's not for your wife
I'll assemble it for free.'

So there we are, problem solved,
though it wasn't very cheap,
the cage should keep the wildlife out
for at least another week.

13: A turn around the garden

I'll just take a turn round the garden
before I have my tea.
The missus usually hands me a cuppa
out there at half past three.

The garden, it ain't very big you know,
just a dozen paces by ten,
a circuit takes less than a minute
before I walk around it again.

The views, they're somewhat restricted,
I can't see over the fence,
but the flowers my missus has planted
are beginning to make some sense.

There are bluebells filling one corner,
lavender creeps to the door,
a clematis climbs up the drainpipe -
I'm not sure that's what drainpipes are for!

So I'll make my afternoon circuit
and see what I can find,
you're welcome to come and join me,
but you'll have to walk behind.

Ten circuits will make my head spin,
but they keep me fit as a flea,
at least that is what I tell my wife
when she brings me my cup of tea.

There's a trench appearing in the lawn,
perhaps I should change my route
to even the surface of the once-lush turf
now scarred by a size ten boot.

But first I'll sit with my PG Tips,
no fancy Earl Grey for me;
a chocolate digestive would go down well
if I can dunk it in my tea.

I shall dream of other walks I made
in the time before Lockdown.
Walks on hills so far away
from any slumbering town.

Walks on winding footpaths,
walks along country lanes,
walks among distant mountains
with unpronounceable names.

There were fun-filled walks with the family
when both our girls were small,
we'd pitch our tent in a meadow
and listen to raindrops fall.

Walking's in our genes I guess,
it's always been the same.
I'd rather be out walking
although I'm growing lame.

Oh dear, I'm getting all wistful,
the wife says I'm becoming a pain,
so I'll finish my well-earned refreshment
and take a turn round the garden again.

14: One foot in front of the other

One foot in front of the other,
that's all it takes to walk.
One foot in front of the other;
most of us do it before we can talk.
One foot in front of the other
then you let go your mother's hand
and the next thing you know, you're off on your own
to explore a wonderland.

A wonderland is everywhere.
It could be at home in your garden or park.
A wonderland is the place where you go
when you're tucked up asleep in the dark.
A wonderland's what you wish it to be
and where you'd like to be found,
gazing into the distance
that responds with seductive sound.

Unusual sounds and unknown sites
are part of wonderland's appeal,
for they convert the magic of mystery
into something you find is real.
So stand on your feet and get out there
and you'll be amazed at what you discover
in the world that becomes your oyster
when you place one foot in front of the other.

15: In a spin

A map, a compass and a GPS,
a gizmo on my smartphone
and I'm still in such a mess.
I've read the blessed guidebook
from the front page to the back
and I still don't know which way to go,
my wife gives me such flak.

There's a signpost in the farmyard,
a waymark on the gate,
there are signs on every fencepost
and the guidebook's up to date.
But footpaths stray both here and there,
I don't know which is mine.
I guess I ought to try each one,
but there's really not much time.

This walk's become a nightmare,
I was lost right from the start.
I should have told her right away,
but hadn't got the heart.
So we're going round in circles
wondering what to do,
and the only good thing I can say
is we have a splendid view.

There's sun on distant water -
A river? Or the sea?
My guidebook gives no hint of this,
so which one can it be?
I think I see a village
a mile or two away,
but what's it doing over there?
The guidebook doesn't say.

I'm lost, I tell you, truly lost
where did I park the car?
If I knew the answer
I'd have an idea where we are.
But everything's a mystery,
my head is in a spin
so my navigation gizmos
are now destined for the bin.

My wife then takes the guidebook
and holds it to the light.
The face that's been despairing
suddenly comes bright,
for the pages I'd been studying
are all dog-eared and bent.
This guide's to Walking in Sussex,' she says
'what we need is Walking in Kent.'

16: The didgeridoo

On a hot December Monday
on the heights of New South Wales,
we heard a curious humming
like hollow trees in autumn gales.
And there an Aborigine was sitting on the ground
blowing through a didgeridoo –
it was that which made the sound.

Fast forward now a dozen years
We were among the Hampshire Downs,
on our way to the Devil's Humps,
though mist was swirling round.
We reached the highest of the humps
with a vague hope that we might
see beyond Chichester Harbour
to the distant Isle of Wight.

Not so, the mist was far too dense,
but we'd seen that view before
and were well content just being there
despite the little we saw.
Emerging through the mist
there came a woman all alone,
with a look upon her smiling face
that said she felt at home.

'Hi', she said, 'don't you love this place
despite a lack of view?
I come here often as I can,
I guess that you do too.'
'You're local then?' I answered,
'from what you have to say,'
'I was until five years ago,
but then we moved away.

We come back every year though,
my hubby George and me,
collecting lengths of dead wood
from a favourite old yew tree.
It's perfect for the work he does,
and you can bet that I come too,
but I know you'll be surprised to hear
he makes the didgeridoo.'

'The didgeridoo? I questioned,
'how did that come about?
Just the very thought of it
fills my mind with doubt.'
'I know,' she said, 'you're not alone
in wondering if it's true,
So I'll tell you George's story
and leave it up to you.

The first time that I met him
he was nothing but a mess,

drugs and drink, that sort of thing,
a man with no address.
I became his social worker
and cleaned him up at last,
then walked him to this hilltop
where the view left him aghast.

He stood here as a broken man,
and then began to cry,
when he realised that there were
better ways to get a 'high.'
I hugged him on this hilltop
and felt a surge of love
as a ray of summer sunshine
beamed upon us from above.

We ran away to Dartmoor
to a rented caravan,
where George found work in the neighbourhood
as a trusted handy man.
When work was scarce he'd take some wood
to see what he could do,
and then one day discovered
he had made a didgeridoo.

We display his work at craft fairs
from spring to Christmas time,
and now he has a website
he sells some of them online.

He's had orders from Australia,
I promise this is true
for my hubby George is now
a master of the didgeridoo.

You couldn't make it up,' she said,
this lady by my side,
'His life's been one of ups and downs,
a mostly bumpy ride.
But where there's love there's always hope,
that's why I'm telling you
my George's life was turned around,
thanks to this hilltop view.'

17: An owl around midnight

Have you seen the owl whose home is in the old oak tree?
I can't believe it saves its awesome beauty just for me.
I've seen it on a fencepost, I've seen it by the barn,
I've seen it gliding low and graceful right around the farm.
I've heard its cry at nightfall with the rising of the moon,
A cry that's not like 'Twit-tawoo' but screeching out of tune.
Its heart-shaped face is handsome, its breast a creamy down,
its eyes alert and piercing though they wear a constant frown.
With golden wings and light-brown head it feeds on mice and voles
and any foolish creatures that should dare desert their holes.

One time when out exploring the South Downs scenic trails
We walked not just on hilltops, but in old romantic vales.
Directed to a meadow we were shown where we could sleep
if we didn't mind the silence – and a flock of downland sheep.
So we pitched our tent beneath an oak, a beechwood curving round,
and thanked our lucky stars for the sanctuary we'd found.
The evening sun slid to the west, and up came half a moon
to herald night's arrival with a Barn Owl's rasping tune.
On and on the screeching went to deny us any rest
but we cursed not its disturbance, for we knew
that we'd been blessed.

Blessed I say, and mean it too, for guess what happened next;
of a sudden all went quiet as the owl came down to rest.
It landed on our two-man tent just inches from our eyes,
we held our breath and gazed in admiration and surprise.

The bird was backlit by the moon, its outline sharp and clear,
we could almost count its feathers – it really was that near.
Life was put on hold that night, we hoped it wouldn't end
for it seemed we'd been away for years and bumped into a friend,
a friend that we would ne'er forget, whose presence was serene
so we drank in every image of that blissful summer scene.

There are moments in each life, they say, as big as one whole year
and so it was that Barn Owl night we cherish now so dear.
A sacred moment, so it seems, to both of us this day,
its memory we two agree will never go away.
Now each time I see a Barn Owl or hear its screeching cry
I recall that downland meadow and a half-moon in the sky,
the beechwood and the oak tree, dew settling on the grass
and the tent pole buckling gently with our feathered
friend's firm grasp.
All these things enriched our lives as you have no doubt guessed,
so I'll repeat it one more time: I know that we've been blessed.

18: The surprise of the familiar

It was there before me every day,
I knew it through and through.
I'd recognise each feature
in that great expansive view.
From farthest east to farthest west
then fading into blue,
while waiting for tomorrow's dawn
to freshen it anew.

I'd rest my chin on weary hands
and gaze upon the scene,
the meadows and the woodlands,
a dozen shades of green,
The old ponds draped with willows,
so restful and serene
each one gathered memories
of the places I had been.

I loved that view in winter time
when carpeted with snow,
I loved it in the springtime too
with bluebells all on show.
I loved it in the summer
when the hay was cut in rows,

but best of all was autumn
with the golden leaves aglow.

I'd been away in distant lands,
I'd seen amazing things,
explored high mountain wilderness
where no bird ever sings.
I'd celebrate the moment,
the gifts that each day brings
while thoughts of home stayed with me
for that's where my heart clings.

I came back home and all was still,
I barely heard a sound.
I held my breath and listened,
then slowly turned around.
The world, my world was not the same,
for all at once I found
that in my weeks of absence
the view I'd loved had drowned.

Down there in the valley
with its meadows and its trees,
its minor hills and hollows
with their flowers and their bees,
the ponds that I would skate across
with every winter freeze,
all were hidden from me
by mists that looked like seas.

But then across this ocean
so many miles away,
a blue-remembered line of hills
stood out on display.
My eyes remained upon them
for they took my breath away
the surprise of the familiar
added magic to my day.

19: The call

It sounds with every springtime song
and lasts all summer through.
It's there with every autumn gale,
the frosts of winter too.
It's there on every raincloud
and with the setting sun,
then rides across the sky at night
from star to star, each one.

It grows among the meadow grass,
it's ageless like the trees.
It sounds like distant thunder
and smells like summer seas.
It's there with every flower,
with every bird that sings;
it's there with every pattern
on a butterfly's soft wings.

Do you hear it? Can you feel it?
Does it resonate with you?
Does your heart beat to its rhythm
with every hard-won view?
Does it fill each sleeping moment
as the soundtrack to your dreams
and remain with you throughout the day,
the driver of your schemes?

If so, then you and I are one
to feel the urge to roam,
an urge that has no disrespect
for those who stay at home.
'Out there's' the place where I belong,
each day I feel the same,
for out there comes an urgent voice -
it's calling me again.

It calls me with a whisper,
it has no need to shout.
Its voice is soft and gentle
as it tries to lure me out.
I won't resist, I haven't yet
I gave in long ago,
and now I'm left with memories
and a heart that's all aglow.

20: Not silence, but peace

There's no such thing as silence, unless maybe you're deaf
for where there's life there's sound of sorts, or else the world's bereft.
We build our homes and spend our lives with bustle and with noise
and ignore the precious benefits of peace that it destroys.
We're deafened by the din of life, created without real cause,
until a desperate need for peace entices us outdoors.

Get far away from road and rail, from factory, city, town,
and turn your back on all the stress that only pulls you down.
Clear your head of everything, all the nonsense you were taught
for an empty brain enables you to start again from naught.
Silence has no meaning while blood runs through your veins
yet peace, true peace, is without a doubt one of life's real gains.

A search for this may lead you to a wilderness of stone
where you'll stumble in the barren lands, both lost and all alone.
There are no signs of mankind here, it's Genesis once more
so cast your soul to heaven's grace and see what there's in store
Just hold your breath and settle down upon a wayside rock
and wait to hear the distant hum of wilderness unlock.

I've heard that hum a thousand times, its creation bears no trace
for it comes from somewhere way out there, a tranquil unknown place.
There may be nothing moving, not even in the air
though your head may now be spinning as your
eyes search everywhere.

That hum consists of voiceless things, of whispers without words
as piercing to the listener as the cry of ladybirds.

You'll hear it now in daylight hours, it becomes a constant theme.
You'll hear it in the night-time too for it powers every dream.
You'll look up to the heavens where the anthem of the stars
says that silence is elusive as the atmosphere of Mars.
So search no more for silence, 'tis of deafness that it speaks,
instead feel free to celebrate the precious gift of peace.

Peace is not an absence of any kind of sound,
it's filled with all the beauty that Nature spreads around.
Peace exists within you, it gathers round the heart
and fills the empty spaces left when troubles all depart.
There's harmony in Nature, it echoes from the moon
and invites each single one of us to hum its restful tune.

21: The quest

He set out as a young man, with just a rough idea
of what his life was missing, though he wasn't really clear.
So without a straight objective he was confused right from the start,
a young man with a lively brain and wildly beating heart.

He stood before shop windows, he stared through open doors,
and then he dreamed of sailing off to distant foreign shores.
He studied pictures, read the books, he quizzed some wise men too
but each answer he received was 'That's entirely up to you.'

Stubble grew upon his chin, his complexion lost its sheen
as his searching went from place to place, listing all he'd seen.
He saw the Taj by moonlight, the pyramids, the Nile.
He saw St Mark's in Venice and the Mona Lisa's smile.
He climbed the highest mountains, he sailed the roughest seas,
he was bitten by mosquitoes and caught a dread disease.

His hair went grey, he grew a beard, with age he went quite lame,
but his search remained consistent, the end was still the same
that all-elusive answer to the questions he'd once had
when leaving home the world to roam when no more than a lad.

One day he woke and with surprise found no more urge to roam,
so turned his back on all things new and made his way back home
where he found the answer to his quest – it had always
been right there:
if you go in search of beauty, you'll find it everywhere.

22: The traveller

If you think that I'm a Luddite you should meet my good friend Jim,
who lives alone in two small rooms of a dilapidated inn.
There was a time the public bar was full of working men
but it's not been used for many years since, oh, I don't know when.

Jim thought so little of it, he let the place run down,
to him the best about it was its location out of town.
He has no television, no radio or car,
as for a phone or laptop, they're a step or two too far.

I first met him in 'sixty-six in a smart Alpine resort.
He seemed to me a quiet man in philosophic thought.
I'd see him in the corner of a favourite pub of mine,
sitting with his cigarettes and a bottle of red wine.

He took some time to open up, but at last began to talk,
so I took him up the valley on my favourite mountain walk.
The wonders that he saw that day unlocked the inner Jim,
and I'm proud to say it could have been the making of him.

In the days and weeks that followed he began to build a dream
of seeing all the world he could, so constructed him a scheme.
He worked hard and he saved hard, he even gave up wine,
and then one day he told me, 'I'm off now, it's my time.'

He said he'd keep in touch with me, and what he said was true,
for once a month a letter or a postcard would come through.

He wrote of distant places, he'd describe each hard-won view,
he wrote of dodgy folk he met, and tales of derring-do.

He almost starved in Africa, but bananas saved his life,
he met a girl in Bali who wished to be his wife.
He visited New Zealand and then went on to Oz
where he thought he'd cross the Outback, why? Well, just because…

Unconcerned with luxury he'd doss down anywhere
and hitch a ride on passing trucks if he hadn't got the fare.
He manned a tug that went aground in the Amazon one day,
at dusk the mozzies drove him mad when they all came out to play.

He saw the world, and then some more and letters still came through
describing lands I'd never see, and some I thought I knew.
He never tired of travelling, he loved life on the road,
recording his adventures on the winding trails he strode.

He's old now. Well, we both are, but still we keep in touch
as once a month the letters come that I enjoy so very much.
But for three months now there's been no news, and as he's all alone,
I take the car and hope by chance to find him in his home.

It's dark when I arrive there, the building looks quite grim.
I bang upon the front door, but there's no response from Jim.
I find a key beneath a brick and make my way inside,
the man may be reclusive, but he surely wouldn't hide.
I strike a light and look around, and then begin to smile
when a note upon the table says:
I'm off to buy some stamps and might be gone for quite a while.

23: Where the wild winds blow

Have you scrambled over mountains
where no man has been before,
have you heard the wild wind
scything through the glen?
Have you felt the pulse of Nature,
known you'd not resist its draw?
Then my son you are the richest of all men.

Have you sat upon a summit
and watched the sunset blaze,
while lost valleys disappeared into the night?
Have you squinted in the noonday sun
on burning summer days,
and polished every star that shone at night?

Have you dared the wildest rapids
on a raft you made of logs?
Were your ragged clothes then soaked
right through and through?
Were you washed ashore a-gasping
then looked up to thank the gods?
Then my son, you know that I am proud of you.

Have you trod the polar ice cap
and been frozen to the bone,

has the black of frostbite chewed away your skin?
Have you staggered lost and lonely
when you're far away from home,
but survived it with a wry but honest grin.

Have you fought your way through jungles,
have you trekked the desert sands?
Have you seen so much that you will never tell?
Have you faced each savage challenge
that you found in foreign lands,
and imagined one could never live so well?

Don't you know the wild you're searching for is never far away?
Don't you know it's just out there and it is free?
Don't you know the world's great wonders
can be conjured up each day?
So come on in, my restless son,
and share it all with me.

24: Above the clouds

Way above the valley and its bustling tourist crowds
the mountain hut stood all alone upon a sea of clouds.
The views were quite exquisite, they stretched from here to there,
a world above the world it was, with lots of sweet fresh air.

If heaven's in a view, they said, then this is Paradise,
a simple palace made of wood among the rock and ice.
It drew the cognoscenti, who came from far and wide
to be above the fluffy clouds and there a night reside.

Agile climbers brave and bold,
they gathered as did grey and old
mountaineers whose summits won
had raised their arms towards the sun.
Hearts uplifted, eyes ablaze
now rested in the noonday shade.

The warden was a friendly guy
who lived above the fog,
and every night he served his guests
the ultimate spag bog.
He knew each crag and each route too,
he'd climbed them all, some old, some new,
but now content to sit and stare,
he lived his days without a care.

One day he had some news to tell,
but feared it might not go down well:
'The mayor decreed you can't go down,
coronavirus is in town
You'll have to stay up here with me.
How long? you ask, we'll have to see,
a day, a week, a month or two –
who knows how I'll put up with you!'

That summer was a sunny one,
but climbers fell out, one by one.
Stuffy dorms with windows shut,
snorers with an upset gut
and endless plates of hot spag bog
thought fit now only for a dog.
Creaking woodwork, squeaking floors,
a basic toilet perched outdoors,
Enough to make an old man sigh
for simple pleasures long gone by.

Climbers dreamed of other places,
wistful looks adorned their faces.
Rocky peaks and snowy passes,
trails that wound through alpine grasses,
streams and lakes and cascades too,
and huts that had a different view.
All these thoughts filled waking hours
like springtime's glut of April showers.

One night I heard a mournful cry,
'I'll trek the Alps before I die.'
Another yearned for Dolomites,
for sunlit mountains without ice.
Eiger, Mönch and Jungfrau too,
somewhere with a different view,
somewhere far from Paradise,
somewhere different, somewhere nice.

Grown men wiped their watery eyes
with thoughts of leaving Paradise.
What once had called them from afar
no longer had its Advent star,
and as the hut had lost its glory,
became the villain of our story,
restless thoughts sowed desperate seeds
leading to some reckless deeds.

On Monday just as dawn was breaking
one crept out, his limbs still aching,
put his rucksack on his back
and gently raised the hut door latch,
said a heartfelt prayer out loud –
then bravely stepped upon the cloud!
He should have plunged then to his doom,
but no, that fate was far too soon.

This cloud it felt like winter's snow,
he knew then he had far to go.

Off to places yet unknown,
mountains where the wild winds moan,
huts in unexpected places,
routes to make on great north faces.
The world's all mine – all mine, he thought,
I'll be a pioneer of sorts.

Other climbers saw his tracks,
grabbed their boots and old rucksacks
then strode off too across the cloud,
amazed that this should be allowed.
From peak to pass they wound their way
on this the most momentous day.
They turned their backs on Paradise
and forgot its magic in a trice.

Back in our hut above the cloud,
the warden shook his head and frowned.
I should have told them weeks ago,
he said his face now all aglow.
It's safe to go down when they pleased,
it's not coronavirus – someone sneezed.

25: Six years

For six years he worked in an office,
I'd prefer not to tell you where,
but he'd check in at nine on a Monday
and spend the rest of the week in despair.
He wasn't born to be stuck indoors,
he needed to feel the breeze,
Needed to watch the clouds float by,
to be among the fields and the trees.

For six years in that jail of an office
he failed to see the sky,
but heard the hum of long strip lights
as the days dragged slowly by,
The clickety-clack of keyboards,
shrill buzz of a telephone's ring,
were alien sounds to this young man's ears,
for whom the days were grim.

For six years in that office
he planned to make his escape.
He needed to be who he was meant to be,
before it became too late.
Weekends gave a hint of heaven,
he'd have gone crazy if not for them,
but Saturday soon became Monday
and he was back in that office again.

For six years in that jail of an office,
he saw others who'd been there for years.
They never complained the way he complained,
nor appreciated his fears.
Now I'm sure there are some who will read this,
who'll say 'What's he moaning about?
If life in that office was purgatory,
why not say 'That's it' and get out?'

I tell you - six years in that office
could have easily turned into ten,
but he heard the call of the wilderness,
the mountains and the glens.
So strong the call, so enticing the sound
it refused to leave him alone
that he went to his boss and told him straight,
'That's it – I'm going home!'

The home he said he was going to,
had different walls and no doors.
The ceiling was one vast heavenly sky
that covered the world outdoors.
There was no safety-net pension,
no pay cheque to help with the rent,
no Council Tax to worry about
when living in a tent.

He'd wander to far-flung places,
he'd always be out and about

experiencing things that he'd dreamed of,
until his money ran out.
He could hardly remember the life that he'd led
in that office so long ago,
for now he'd landed a season's work
among mountains covered with snow.

When snow disappeared in the springtime,
he worked looking after some sheep
that grazed the rich green pastures
on which at night he would sleep.
The seasons went by one by one,
much faster than before
when he'd found himself trapped for six long years
behind that office door.

A simple life was all he sought,
his needs were very small:
some food in his belly a clear mountain view,
and somewhere to sleep – that's all.
The call of the wild remained with him
and ensured he was never lost,
while those he once knew in that office
wondered if he was counting the cost.

No - I'm sure that he wasn't,
for I met him when he had grown old,
a ragged-looking fella
who'd survived the wind and the cold.

He had a glow about him,
his head still full of dreams,
then he drifted into the setting sun
and vanished among the moonbeams.

26: A friend indeed

Our friendship lasted thirty years,
well, thirty years and more
though he had a level of intellect
I'd never known before.
He'd been a mathematician
with a lively questioning brain,
Me? I'm the village idiot
but he treated everyone the same.

He was twenty years my senior,
he'd led an interesting life,
he had two brainy offspring
and a professor for a wife.
On retirement he was editor
of a journal for which I'd write
and we met to discuss a feature
one damp November night.

Mountains brought us together,
a passion for books as well,
and as our friendship deepened,
what stories he would tell!
There were peaks that we had both climbed,
and valleys we'd explored,
there were travel books we both had read
and writers we adored.

His active days were over
by the time that we first met,
but he became my inspiration
for some climbs he'd not forget.
There was one in Val di Mello
he longed to visit yet again,
so he travelled out to Italy
where I met him off the train.

You'd think the Alps of Italy
would shimmer in the sun,
but not on this occasion
they hid themselves, each one.
Clouds hung low on treetops,
the rain cascaded down,
but none of this concerned my friend
who refused to wear a frown.

It was there he had his birthday,
eighty years, would you believe!
This polymath who'd become my friend
with his heart spread on his sleeve.
A large polenta al fungi
we ate in pouring rain,
and drank his health from plastic cups,
then drank his health again!

All that was many years ago,
my friend has passed away,

but the gifts his friendship gave me
are with me to this day.
He showed all men are equal
despite their size of brain,
for kindness and a love of life
make all mankind the same.

27: Heaven's door

Seven hundred metres above the valley floor
there stands a group of stone-built huts I've visited before.
As old as time itself they seem standing in a row,
baked by years of summer sun, or hid by winter's snow.
In blissful isolation, backed by the highest trees
and brushed by every scent that's carried by the breeze,
lived in by the farmers for three months every year
their doorways are like heaven's door with Paradise so near.

You'll hear a stream go chuckling past, you'll hear each
bird that sings,
you'll hear the grazing cattle and every bell that rings.
You'll hear the beating of your heart, the marmot's warning cry
when it spies a golden eagle hanging in the sky.
All else you'd say was silent, but I tell you it's not so
for the busy hum of life itself is something you should know.
All these things belong up here, among the stone-built huts
worn by time and smoothed by hands that have the common touch.

It takes a lot of effort to get there, I must say,
a lot of sweat and panting breath no matter what the day.
But every step is worth it, every drop of sweat worthwhile
for when you look around you, you're guaranteed to smile.
The mountains are majestic with their fields of melting snow,
the granite peaks when stained with gold by evening's alpenglow,
the chestnut woods below you, the huddled village too,
this timeless Alpine world in which it seems there's nothing new.

I've known this alp for fifty years, I found it when alone.
I've sat there with each farmer in his simple wood-smoked home.
I've been there in the mornings when the cows were being milked
and placed the lids upon the churns to stop it being spilled.
I once was there at twilight when they'd smoke their evening pipes
and dreamy-eyed imagined theirs to be the perfect life.
But when the storm clouds gather and lightning's all around
I've felt the huts' foundations shake upon once solid ground.

One time I wrote about this alp, it was published in a book
along with lots of Alpine photographs I took.
But no words in my thesaurus could in any way describe
the joy that fills each part of me and makes me come alive
whenever I draw near this place I treasure as if mine
and I'd gladly take you there with me, but just one at a time.

28: Three in one

The sun came up three times one day,
tho' many years ago.
I saw it with my own two eyes
when high on Austrian snow
where I was leading wanderers
from peak to blissful peak
throughout that glorious summer,
for seven days a week.

Those wanderers I was leading
were young and fit and bold.
Even I was agile then, - not now
I'm much too old.
I lived each day as if the last
with no thought of tomorrow,
and scrambled up each crystal peak,
knowing they would follow.

One time I offered two of them
adventure of their own,
to climb a local mountain,
just the three of us alone.
We left our valley hostelry
with stars our only light
to find our way as best we could
throughout that secret night.

At last we reached the summit
with its lofty snow-dashed crown
where we pulled on extra clothing,
then tried to settle down.
Our teeth they chattered with the cold,
and all stayed wide awake,
high above the valley,
above our village and its lake.

At four o'clock that morning
we saw a distant glow.
It could only be the rising sun
on far-off Alpine snow.
It then popped us so suddenly
it caught us by surprise,
spreading wonder on each face,
and dazzling in our eyes.

'Now come with me,' I urged my friends,
'as quickly as you can'
and down the summit snowfield
all three of us then ran.
Losing height we lost the sun,
the morning lost its light.
The day was poised in mystery
that was neither day nor night.

Then up it came, that sun again,
rising in the east,

flooding all below it –
an amazing visual feast.
Twice now we'd watched the day appear,
and we'd see it one more time
if we scrambled down the rocks below –
with caution we'd be fine.

And so it was, three times that day
we relished each new dawn,
knowing we'd been truly blessed
to see the world reborn.
But there was one more gift in store,
it's one I didn't know,
for standing in a meadow
was an old farm, all aglow.

Aglow it was with daybreak's sun,
its blackened timbers gleamed,
while at the door a woman stood,
she saw us and she beamed.
'Grüss Gott' she said, 'where have you been?
It's so early in the day.
I suppose you've watched the sun rise –
would you like to stay?'

'I have some home-made bread and jam,
some coffee and some cheese.
Franz and I have plenty,
so won't you join us – please?

We don't see many wanderers,
    they rarely come this way
so if you'll share our breakfast
you will surely make our day.'

Franz had been a-milking
    his four bell-clattering cows,
and carried two large shining cans
        back towards the house.
The five of us now shared their feast
    as birds sang in the trees,
    the songs of Alpine summers
        drifting on the breeze.

I looked the lady in the eye
    and knew she was content.
Yet her hands were both arthritic,
    her fingers mostly bent.
Franz was strong despite his age,
    he clearly loved his wife.
    The two of them together
with an idyllic way of life.

'It's not yet six o'clock,' I said,
    'and you've been up and out,
    while down there in the valley
they're still sleeping, there's no doubt.'
    'My dear,' she said and placed
    her tiny hand upon my arm.

'We have no clock in our abode –
the sun is our alarm.'

Well, all that really happened
more than fifty years ago.
But the memories remain as fresh
as crisp high Alpine snow.
Each sunrise that we saw that day
was indeed a special gift,
while breakfast with the farmer's wife
gave each of us a lift.

Call me an old romantic,
I won't deny it's so,
for I savour every moment
from those years of long ago.
If adventures were worth living once,
they're worth living one more time,
so I wait in expectation
for each new day's sun to shine.

29: Blame global warming

I know a mountain restaurant, Stieregg is its name,
It rests behind the Eiger on a bank of old moraine,
A meadow of the sweetest grass where alpine flowers grow,
An oasis in a wilderness of rock and ice and snow.

Dwarfed by massive mountains – the Fiescherhorn is one,
It offers light refreshment and shade from summer's sun.
Sheep graze in the pasture, marmots burrow deep,
It is the most idyllic spot in which you'd ever sleep.

A narrow path above a gorge takes just about an hour,
And every step reminds you of the mountains' untamed power.
With Grindelwald behind you, ahead the dizzy heights,
The Oberland seduces with its numerous delights.

The restaurant we're going to has been there many years
But the meadow that it stands on is less safe than it appears,
You see the permafrost that glues the huge wall of moraine
Is melting at a rapid rate, helped by the sun and rain.

Each year I make my visit - alone or with some friends,
I fear collapse is coming, that's what Nature now intends,
All thanks to global warming (the same as climate change)
You can see it very clearly in every mountain range.

The last time that I went there I was shocked by what I found,
The meadow Stieregg stood upon was losing lots of ground,

The mountain wall above it was devoid of ice and snow
And where glaciers once were plentiful was little left to show.

The restaurant was just as good as it had ever been
But I couldn't help but mourn the changing mountain scene.
The Alps were shrinking year by year, of that there was no doubt
With the evidence of rockfall lying all about.

Then I received a message telling me just what I'd feared,
Stieregg and its meadow that June had disappeared.
I know I'd seen it coming, the warning signs were clear
But I'd hope to visit one more time, later on that year.

The path that teetered on the gorge has nowhere now to go,
Stieregg's just a memory along with ice and snow.
I'm so lucky that I knew it in those blissful far-off days
When I'd look up to the mountains and sing their rightful praise.

Well, that was then and this is now, the years have scurried by
And the signs of global warming beam from every summer sky.
Glaciers shrink and snowfields melt, rocks hurtle to the ground,
Climate change is everywhere, just listen to its sound.

It's possible that Stieregg is just a name to you.
It's possible you've never gazed upon its stunning view.
The lowlands we inhabit are unlike a mountain range,
But you and I should not ignore this rapid climate change.

30: A cavern of ice

His name was Marcus Clerici,
he was bright-eyed, mopped-headed and Swiss,
I met him many years ago when we both worked in St Moritz.
He wasn't the brightest of buttons, education much poorer than mine,
but he could get away with murder the way that his eyes would shine.

If work was something that had to be done,
he'd find someone else to do it,
often that someone turned out to be me, and everybody knew it.
Sometimes we'd ski together at three thousand metres and more
and only return to the valley when the light went at half past four.

At night-time we'd take the sleds out and have a race in the dark,
whizzing downhill through the snowbound woods,
having a bit of a lark.
One night we hurtled a bit too fast as we approached the River Inn,
where Marcus came a cropper and with a cry fell head-first in.

Now one thing that Marcus was good at was
hot dogs with sauerkraut,
so on special festive occasions
he'd get his home-made barbecue out.
It was then he'd make a killing serving hot dogs by the score,
and when he was running short of rolls
I'd rush off and get him some more.

A ski jump competition took place every winter time,
when Marcus would sell his hot dogs
and glasses of steaming gluhwein.
'I'd like you to help me prepare,' he said, 'I have a great idea.
We'll dig us a cave from the snow and ice
that builds up every year.'

So we took a shovel and pickaxe
and began hacking away at the ice,
but for every shovelful Marcus took out, I'd use the pickaxe twice.
We sweated with the effort, though the temperature was way below,
as beside the cave we created grew an enormous pile of snow.

At some time in the afternoon a well-heeled couple came by,
'Mein Gott what are you doing?' I heard a German voice cry.
'Are you trying to build a mountain, or are you taking one down?
I've never seen such a mighty heap,
you could almost bury the town.'

Marcus stopped his digging while I just carried on
fearing we were in trouble - if so what had we done wrong?
But Marcus simply rubbed his neck and gave that crafty smile
then leaned upon his shovel for just a little while.

'I don't know how to say this,' said Marcus with a frown,
'My friend here left his car last night
when the battery let him down.
It was then we had that dump of snow, the worst we've had so far.
As you can see we're now working hard

to locate his buried car.'
'Mein Gott' the German said once more, 'that really is bad news.
A motor car is far too precious for a man to lose.
I'd like to help you find it, but I've too much on today.
Good luck, may God be with you,' then he turned and scuttled away.

31: My friend Fred

This is the tale of my friend Fred Malone,
he hails from Alaska, that's when he's at home.
We met on a Swiss alp, I remember the date
t'was a warm summer Sunday in the year Eighty-eight.

He took off his hat, wiped the sweat from his brow,
gave a gappy-toothed grin, I recall it right now.
Then he said 'Say young man, why don't you sit,
take in the view, chew the cud for a bit.'

So I sat down beside him right there on the grass,
pondered a moment, and then turned to ask
'Are you here with some friends, or perhaps all alone?'
It was then that he told me his name: Fred Malone.

Now Fred was a legend, I knew very well,
stories about him I'd often heard tell,
tales of the wilderness where he'd made his home
in an old-fashioned cabin he'd built on his own.

The cabin now stood on the shores of a lake.
He'd chosen the site for the fish that he'd take
each day for his supper to cook on a grill
before washing it down with a drink from his still.

'I play the pianee' he suddenly said.
'I got it from Grandpa, once he was dead.

I then took it home with a horse and a sleigh
when the lake was all frozen one cold winter's day.'

'Those winters are hard, I want you to know,
and often they drop to forty below.
But imagine the beauty of those frozen nights
when the skies are alive with the green Northern Lights.

'I live thirty miles or so from a town
so I'll play me some music should moods get me down.
But you know my young friend it ain't happened yet
I don't have a dull moment to sit and to fret.

But I'll tinkle the iv'ries any time that I please -
just imagine Tchaikovsky adrift in the breeze!
And I've also got books, two dozen maybe
that I read out loud, some include poetry.'

I imagined him then with his hand-me-down clothes,
completely content with the life that he chose.
He was, it seemed, a man of extremes
whose lifestyle was built on the back of some dreams.

I then dared to say 'I've a question for you,
What brought you out here? Surely not just the view?'
'Well no,' he then grinned, 'I thought what the heck,
while I've still got some puff I'll go for a trek.'

'So where are you going today, may I ask?'
'I'm headed up there,' he said, 'over that pass

where I aim to sleep in an old mountain inn.
Hey – why don't you join me?' he asked with a grin.

So off we went slowly, we two stride by stride,
'til we got to the pass where we stood side by side.
Fred took in the view, and gazed all about.
'Tis a bootiful world,' he said, 'of that there's no doubt.'

Six days Fred and I trekked on Switzerland's hills.
Six days when we cured all society's ills.
Six days of magic with an extraordinary man,
those days remain with me as memories can.

The day that we parted I looked in his eye,
knowing our friendship no money could buy.
'I'll drop you a line', he said, 'if I might.
Our time in these mountains has been a delight.'

Fred returned to Alaska, I went home to my wife
and told her about the old man and his life.
We then read all the letters he sent from his home
to discover how happy he was all alone.

He told of the nights when he heard the wolves howl.
He told us of caribou, and the haunting of owls.
He described the rich berries he'd make into pies
and the music that sometimes put tears in his eyes.

He told us the dangers of bears with their cubs,
and the way he'd created an outdoors hot tub.

He told of a life that to us was serene,
and described like a poet the things that he'd seen.

I once planned to make a film about him.
I wanted to capture his warm-hearted grin.
I wanted to show my friend at his ease,
despite living alone in Nature's deep freeze.

His life I imagined had lessons for all.
There are some things of course you won't learn in a school.
But it wasn't so long before I had found
my plan to film Fred fell on cold stony ground.

When I wrote to tell Fred I confessed I was sad.
'Forget it, my friend, you mustn't feel bad,
there's a reason for most things I'm sure you'll agree.
I'm quite happy to take whatever will be.'

He was a romantic, of that I could tell,
a man whose warm heart could ring like a bell.
Though he lived in a cabin alone by a lake
it was just as he'd planned. It was not a mistake.

So he swatted the mozzies on warm summer nights,
and shivered in winter 'neath bright Northern Lights.
He played his piano by the light of the moon,
and wandered through forest while whistling a tune.

The years drifted by, his correspondence now rare.
There were times when I feared he'd been killed by a bear.

And when I received no more letters from Fred,
I had to conclude that the dear man was dead.

I'll never forget him, he was one of a kind,
and those six days together gave more than you'd find
in a lifetime of searching for one loyal friend,
while Fred Malone's friendship stayed true to the end.

32: The painted mountains

Imagine if you will a mountain deep down in the sea.
Imagine if you can a fish where no fish ought to be.
Imagine if you're able to feel such pressure from below,
that it forces mountains from the sea, and then you watch them grow.

In long-gone Mesozoic times, indeed there was a sea,
in which all kinds of creatures died and then became debris.
They crusted into sediments and formed a coral reef
that submitted to a landmass pressing up from far beneath.

That coral slowly left the sea and turned upon its side
exposing fossil fishes with nowhere left to hide.
The reef became pale mountains reaching up to dizzy heights
that today are known to one and all as the Dolomites.

Great pinnacles of rock rise up before our eyes
each one so amazing it fills us with surprise
slabs and spires, turrets too
concentrate each landscape view.

Two summers I was based there in the shadow of such peaks
taking walkers wandering, each group for just two weeks.
We'd have our breakfast early, then set off on a trail
that every day would lead to scenes of grandeur without fail.

We crossed a dozen passes, we stumbled over screes,
we picnicked in the pastures, anywhere we pleased.

We tiptoed on some ridges, we slid down slopes of snow
and made long lists of all the places we would like to go.

There were lakes in certain valleys turning mountains on their head
and tunnels cut in World War I by soldiers now long dead.
We'd watch thin clouds drift high above us counting off the hours
and marvel at the meadows so full of alpine flowers.

These are the painted mountains – not coloured by a brush
but the ever-changing textures of sunlight's magic flush.
I'd gaze on them at sunrise when the rocks were pink with dawn
and see them washed by shadows of the drifting clouds each morn.

When each summer ended and my groups all headed home
I'd stay a few days longer and wander on my own.
I'd look for new adventures to explore another time
and toast the painted mountains with a glass of local wine.

33: Living on air

When Franz walked from the consultant's room
his heart was heavy with dread,
If the diagnosis was what he'd been told,
in six months he would be dead.
It's not the news he'd been hoping to hear,
and his mind went suddenly blank
as he wandered alone by the riverside,
then found a spare seat on the bank.
Six months, that's all! That's nowhere enough
to do all the things he'd planned,
How can you count your achievements
on the fingers of one hand?
Okay, he'd do what he'd hoped to do,
when his working days would cease,
He'd go back to the mountains
and spend his last days there in peace.
He called his lawyer, signed some forms
and said farewell to his friends
Then stuffed a few clothes in a rucksack,
and some books on which he'd depend.
He gathered his medication
and dropped it all in a bin
then made his way as fast as he could
to his favourite mountain inn.

The berghaus (or inn) he would go to
was more than a century old,

it stood all alone on the edge of a meadow
defying the worst winter cold.
Geraniums hung over window sills,
a water trough spluttered out back,
and the only route to get there
was on a long and winding track.
Franz knew it from his childhood
when he'd discovered the mountains were grand,
iconic summits dashed with snow,
the pride of the Oberland.
They drew him back time after time,
they never let him down,
and daily he would dream of them
in his office in the town.
He recalled the view on arrival
with his parents that very first day
when he thought he'd gone to heaven
and there was no better place to stay.
Now fragile, bewildered and weary
Franz made his painful way there,
but was slowly rejuvenated
as he breathed in the fresh mountain air.

He was given a room with a creaking floor
and a door that refused to shut tight.
But the mattress was soft, the duvet warm,
and a candle stub gave him some light.
There he would make himself a home,
at least for a week or two,

for the lovely old building was noted by all
for its quite remarkable view.
The mountains that he gazed on
were gleaming with late spring snow
and they turned to gold as the sun went down
in the evening alpenglow.
The meadows in which he'd sit and dream
were rich with alpine flowers,
while the distant sound of cowbells
rang throughout the daylight hours.
But when thunder crashed and lightning flashed
it was a very different scene,
for rain beat on the old shingle roof
and swept over it like a stream.
Franz would lean on the window sill
and give a wistful smile,
for all of this he claimed as his –
at least for a little while.

The couple who ran the berghaus
had a waitress with golden hair.
They looked on Franz as a special guest
and gave him extra care,
Though he rarely drank, had little to eat
and slept when his need required,
the way he faced that fate of his
was something the others admired.
The inn was mostly a restaurant
used by locals when day was done

so it wasn't long before our friend
was known by everyone.
When the weather was fine he'd wander outdoors,
watch farmers tossing the hay,
for spring had turned into summer
as fast as night turns to day.
He refused to count the months he'd lived
since he'd left the consultant's room
for he'd rather pass on with a smile on his face
than waste his days with gloom.
While the pain that he'd been living through
diminished with each week
the state of his health was something of which
neither Franz nor innkeeper would speak.

When summer turned into autumn
and Franz was still living there,
he was asked to stand in for the waitress,
the girl with the golden hair.
She'd not had a day-off all summer
and needed a few days' break,
so he served the drinks, he served the food
and even made a cake.
And that's when we first met him,
standing behind the bar,
he greeted us with a friendly smile
and asked if we'd come far.
We told him we were trekking
and needed a bed for the night,

so he showed us to a creaky-floor room
and gave us a candle for light.
Joining us after dinner
we shared our love of the Alps with him,
the much-loved places we'd been to,
and claimed this was our favourite inn.
He said there was much he'd like to see
but was content with just being there,
and not for a single moment
did we imagine his inner despair.

The memory of that berghaus
stayed with us when we went home.
So the following year we went back again,
amazed at how time had flown.
We strode up the track with that view to our back
and heard the cowbells ring,
then left our boots in the boot room
and pushed open the door of the inn.
And there stood Franz with a smile on his face
as he welcomed us back like a friend,
one who had so much more to live,
instead of one facing the end.
He'd gone there eighteen months before
and watched the seasons fly,
and in that time discovered
he was the man who couldn't die.
Of course he never said that,
it was the mountains of which he would speak,

by now he knew every glacier,
every rock face and snow-covered peak.
Then he asked 'How long will you stay here?
I'm the manager now you see.
You'll have the best room in the berghaus
and the finest view comes free!'

Franz clearly loved that berghaus,
with its timbers of weathered pine
and the sense of peace gathered round it
whenever the weather was fine.
Better than all medication
it controlled his pain deep inside,
but one moonlit night his face turned white
with concern he attempted to hide.
'Sorry,' he said as he sweated,
'Indigestion, I've had too much to eat,'
Then scraped his chair legs on the floor
and staggered to his feet.
He was fine the following morning,
our friend with the generous heart,
so we promised to help him pick bilberries
which he could then bake inside a tart.
There were bilb'ries all over the hillside,
their colour a dusty blue,
but every few minutes we'd sit by a bush
just to admire the view.
Our friendship then grew much deeper
as the days went drifting by

and we never imagined one moment
that our friend had gone there to die.

We couldn't go back the following year,
I was sent elsewhere to write.
But we couldn't forget that old mountain inn,
especially at night
when Franz would sit down and join us,
to while away the hours,
and the starlit mountains hung in the sky
beyond the window-sill flowers.
But two years after we'd last been there
we decided to return.
We took a flight to Geneva,
then a comfortable train to Bern.
We strode up the track without looking back,
to the berghaus that Franz called home,
and there was the girl with the golden hair
looking sad as she stood all alone.
'I'm afraid', she said, 'poor Franz is dead,
he went several weeks ago.
Some friends of his brought his ashes here
and cast them on last winter's snow.'
Well, I guess that's the end of my story,
it's not for us to despair,
for Franz went to that berghaus to die,
and his spirit remains up there.

34: Shrinking horizons

For much of my life I travelled the world
with camera and notebook in hand,
having adventures I'd never have dreamed,
in every foreign land.
I've stood on icy summits to photograph the view,
and walked in the steps of Hooker
as he gathered plants for Kew.
I've trekked the mountain deserts
of mysterious Ladakh
whose ancient Buddhist gompas
insisted I went back.
I did, the Indus river sustained the life I found
among the small oases
raising crops on stony ground.
Another time I rode a horse on ridges near Tibet
and gazed on scenes of grandeur
that I never will forget.
Nepal, Bhutan and Sikkim too,
the names slip off my tongue.
That's where I've spent the best of days;
remarkable, each one.

Mount Ararat stands all alone,
Noah's Ark they say is there,
but I saw no sign on my ascent,
in truth I didn't care.
From Turkey off to Russia when still the USSR

to explore the Caucasus Mountains –
that was almost a step too far,
With visa problems when I left,
I feared I'd not get home
but the gods were smiling on me
and I made it on my own.
I went out to the Andes to write of wild Peru,
where some friendly Quechua Indians
showed me where and what to do.
We crossed the highest passes
and camped beneath the stars
and learned to live on mutton
grilled in sunken turf-filled fires.
Our search for Alpamayo was rewarded late one day
when its beauty so enthralled me
I wished that I could stay.

From Norway to Morocco
and most countries in between,
I've forgotten names of half the special places I have seen.
The mountains of the Pyrenees
became a spiritual home,
while through each region of the Alps
I wandered on my own.
Australia and New Zealand also played their part
and in each one I left behind something of my heart.
I'm sorry if this is bragging, it isn't meant to be,
for guilt is like a big black cloud hanging over me.
You see my carbon footprint is something I confess

weighs heavy on my conscience I'm unable to redress.
But horizons now have shrunken,
I guess that yours have too,
and I'm well content to be right here.
I tell you – this will do.

35: Back to the mountains

I must get back to the mountains again,
I've been away far too long,
I wake in the night to their siren lure
reminding me where I belong.
The mountains, their valleys, their grim gorges too,
each one an integral part
of the wild and untamed landscapes
that hold on to my heart.

I must be back among mountains again
where I've spent the best of my years,
the challenges and the rewards they provide
dismiss all my lowland fears.
To walk once more in the shadow of giants,
enticed by glacial streams
that gather among the celestial heights,
the substance of my dreams.

I'd love to be back among mountains again,
where their clusters of low-growing pine
give way to the slabs of sun-warmed rock
on which I used to climb.
Those days may now be behind me,
but I recall each one with a thrill,
and I think of the hard-won summits
whose magic remains with me still.

I feel lost when away from the mountains,
they enriched practically all of my days,
they're the nearest I'll get to paradise –
they were never a passing phase.
I've stood upon peaks and raised up my arms
and even touched heaven's blue,
and mapped in my mind all the country below
stretched out in a summit's view.

My mountain days may be over,
but given the slightest chance
I'll be off again with rucksack and tent
to gain just a moment's glance.
I'll be there in less than a second,
or at least as fast as I can,
there's nothing now that will stop me,
for you see - I'm a mountain man.

36: Along the Pyrenees

Given the fitness, the energy and several weeks free,
I'd trek once again from Ocean to Sea.
I'd start among Basque hills where Atlantic clouds rise
and end in the east among Mediterranean tides.
Truth be told in years gone by I trod most of the trails,
but my lifelong love of the Pyrenees is something that never fails.

Three routes take the trekker from the Ocean to the Sea;
one in France, one in Spain, and a high route – that was for me.
Left foot in France, right foot in Spain I strode the frontier crest,
crossing its peaks and passes, seldom descending to rest.
I trekked the route in stages of two weeks at a time,
and almost lost my way upon some peaks I couldn't climb.

Up there above the valleys, with the eagle and the chough
I'd make my way from dawn to dusk and never have enough.
Have you slept upon a stony bed and counted every star,
and woken in the darkness unsure of where you are?
Well that was my experience on so many moonless nights,
while far off in the foothills I could see a small town's lights.

Sunrise was a blessing as I watched a riotous morn
rise above a cloud sea that delayed the valley's dawn.
Down there in a hotel the guests woke up to rain,
while I would bask in sunshine that cleansed both France and Spain.
Each day was an adventure and I had no thought for ease
as long as I had peaks to climb along the Pyrenees.

There were glaciers, there were snowfields, and rocky spires of stone.
There were meadows in the valleys where once I camped alone.
There were patches of green lichen, and others just like rust
that grew in tiny crevices to form a flaky crust.
Nature's rich diversity drew me year by year,
it filled me with excitement and banished any fear.

There were tadpoles twitching nervously beside some shallow pools.
There were times when I'd be thankful to drink from waterfalls.
There were marmots shrieking loudly, I heard a red deer bark,
and slapped away the midges that descended in the dark.
Most days I'd see an izard (a kind of small wild goat)
with tiny horns and distinctive stripe along its red-brown coat.

Some nights I slept in refuges, ate hearty meals and snacks
and in the morning early heaved my rucksack on my back
to climb again the hillside to the frontier ridge I'd left
where I'd set my compass eastward, for heading east was best.
East would take me onward to the Mediterranean Sea
while I'd wish to keep on wandering, for wandering set me free.

From Lescun I trekked to Gavarnie, an easy stage to love,
I climbed the Maladeta with no higher peaks above
then wandered in a wilderness so different from my home,
where many unnamed passes were marked with cairns of stone.
I trekked in sunshine and in rain, I trembled through a storm,
but every day I gave up prayers of thanks that I'd been born.

East of the Maladeta there's a region without trees,
a land of naked mountains, of water and of screes.

I'd pitch my tent beside a tarn and listen to my heart
saying why not stay forever – don't bother to depart.
'Tis true I found it difficult to drag myself away
but swore that I'd be back again another sunny day.

One time I trekked for seven days and saw no-one at all.
I heard no other voices, no shepherd's distant call.
I sat upon the summits like a noble ruler-king
and listened to the anthems the world alone would sing.
I wanted nothing more than this, for life's riches were all mine,
they'd stay with me for ever, until the end of time.

I never made it to the Med, I stopped near Canigou.
The sun was blazing fiercely from a sky of clearest blue.
Aromatic plantlife tossed its fragrance in the air
and I was overcome with sadness that I would soon be there.
So I turned my back and headed home, at least I still was free
to return once more and conclude that trek from
the Ocean to the Sea.

37: An end and a beginning

If you journey south from Lourdes beside the Gave de Pau,
the mountain torrent guides you just as far as you can go.
Its birth is where the clouds sail by, so high above the screes
that lie beneath the best I know of all the Pyrenees.

The village nearest to it has no architectural grace,
but this hardly matters with the view that's in your face.
The buildings at its entrance together slip away
to reveal a scene of wonder that will hold you there all day.

The first time I was there was in the spring of sixty-nine,
burning with ambition and a list of peaks to climb.
Just names they were 'til then, of course, just marks upon a map
and a border line 'twixt France and Spain with little overlap.

I had a coffee, bought some bread and let the time drift by
while gazing at a mountain wall that held aloft the sky.
My plans were all in tatters now, content I was to dream,
delaying 'til tomorrow my too-ambitious scheme.

But then I heaved my rucksack to my travel-weary back
and made my way towards the church along a well-trod track.
The path continued upward through meadowland and trees
then brought me to a dome of grass where I sank upon my knees.

If heaven's in a view, I thought, then this is surely one.
I'll pitch my tent and settle down, stay here 'til life is done.

Snow lay there in patches, melting through the hours
while the hillside just below me was bright with tiny flowers.

I stayed there for a day or two, that view before my eyes
and from what I say I'm sure you'll guess that I was mesmerised.
The Grande Cascade was over there, born up in the snow
then tumbled in a drift of spray, the longest drop I know.

Summits that were boldly holding sun-warm Spain at bay,
three thousand metre lumps, they were, I'd climb them all one day.
Terraces of snow and ice had lined the mountain wall
and as the sun rose higher I'd hear the avalanches fall.

I made a poor attempt to find the way I'd planned to go,
but everything above my perch was blocked with unsafe snow.
A snow-bridge broke beneath me, I fell into a stream
which told me spring's a crazy time to chase a crazy dream.

That could have been my story's end, for time was running short,
there were other places yet to see, for which I'd had a thought,
each one would give adventures and call me back again
to climb those magic mountains that border France and Spain.

And yet, and yet, I knew by now as years would come and go
I'd return to that great mountain cirque along the Gave de Pau.
Sometimes I'd cross the frontier through a well-known rocky brèche
exchanging Spain's baked moonscape for a scene both bold and fresh.

I'd climb the mountains one by one, make notes of where I'd been,
I'd sleep in all the refuges, I'd bivouac by the stream.

I'd lie awake to count the stars and watch the moon rise too.
I'd find the finest vantage point and celebrate each view.

Yes, the Cirque de Gavarnie is the place of which I write,
I can conjure up its beauty through the day and through the night.
Since the spring of sixty-nine I've always seen it as a friend,
an end and a beginning, not a beginning with an end.

38: The lost mountain

The lost mountain was found many years ago.
Known to the French it's simply Mont Perdu,
to the Spanish, it's Perdido.
This third highest Pyrenean summit,
stands south of the border in Spain.
I climbed it once by its north-east face
and would love to climb it again.

In truth it's not much to look at,
a three thousand metre dome,
but it's what can be seen from the snow on its crown
that I think of when I'm at home.
There's a splay of deep-cut valleys
that slice through the land below,
three exquisite deep canyons
and a beautiful valley on show.

The Pineta flows down to Bielsa,
a village with charm all its own
while the deep Gargantas de Escuain
of the canyons is the least well-known.
Anisclo's a joy to descend into
with its pools of emerald green
and the cascades that fall from the narrowing cliffs
are as good as any I've seen.

But it's Ordesa that wins all the plaudits,
its reputation has spread far and wide,
drained by the Arazas river
walled by immense bands of rock either side.
The thunder of its waterfalls,
the rainbows painted by spray
the beech woods and the pine trees
where the squirrels are seen at play.

Go there in the springtime
when Perdido looks its best,
while its upper snowfields avalanche
and in meadows come to rest.
Wander through the valley when those meadows fill with flowers
or stretch out on a vantage point
to dream away the hours.

Ordesa's far too hot for me
when summer comes around
the crowds arrive in busloads
and destroy its peace with sound.
But go there in October
on a blissful autumn day
and climb the southern cliffside
to the Faja de Pelay.

The Faja is a ledge-like path
six hundred metres high,

it teeters for an hour or more
halfway to the sky.
Ahead the long lost mountain,
the Arazas below
but when you reach its upper end
there's still a way to go.

Lawn-like meadows, waterfalls,
low crags that close its head
suggest more ways to wander on
or trek downstream instead.
Each route will lead to wonderland,
I've followed every one;
I've watched small herds of izard
and been bronzed by autumn's sun.

I've crossed the hidden passes,
I've waded through its streams,
I've loved each expedition
that once were only dreams.
Ordesa may be number one
but none will let you down
for if you raise your searching eyes
the lost mountain will be found.

39: The enchanted mountains

The Sierra de los Encantados, the name slides from the tongue,
sharp ragged peaks and sparkling lakes caressed by Spanish sun.
They're found not far from Espot in the central Pyrenees,
peaks that clothe my sleeping hours and remain all day to tease.

I remember when I first saw them, t'was the summer of Sixty-five,
I was young and fit and full of plans, and one hundred per cent alive.
There was no chance to climb them then, for that I'd have to wait,
but once I breathed their box-fresh air,
that effectively sealed my fate.

The romantic enchanted mountains
(that's what the name really means),
look down on San Maurici's lake, with its pinewoods
and tumbling streams,
Wild boar inhabit the woodlands, pairs of izard roam the screes,
and a tiny mountain refuge sits in a clearing surrounded by trees.

The Sierra de los Encantados are shepherds transformed into stone.
When grazing their flock one Sunday at dawn,
far away from their home
they heard the church bells ringing in the crisp early morning air,
and said 'Let's not bother with Mass today,
we're better off here than there.'

With that, the legend tells us, the two men of whom we speak
in an instant became a mountain, one that has two distinct peaks.
And there they've stood since who knows when,
magnificent they appear,
I swore one day I'd climb them, and I did so one memorable year.

Lost in the mist, they were that day, washed by steady rain.
Should I go back to Espot and hope to return again?
'Oh no' said my friend, 'now that we're here we
might as well stand at their feet'
But the moment we actually touched the rock,
that rain had turned into sleet.

'Let's give it a go,' I heard my friend say,
'Come, tie yourself to the rope'
and as I did I felt a surge of both confidence and hope.
We made our way slowly upward, in the sleet and the sightless gloom
by way of a lengthy dividing crack in which we barely had room.

A few hundred metres higher, the sleet had turned into snow
yet though we had nothing to see in the crack,
we had a good idea where to go.
And then for a very brief moment the wind tore a hole in the cloud,
displaying the lake like a puddle below
with tiny trees gathered around.

'Hurrah' said my friend 'we're almost there, I'll beat you to the top,'
so with snow in our eyes and the joy of surprise we continued
without a stop.

With nothing to see from the shepherd's head,
as more clouds had stolen the view,
we roped our way down in the gloom of the day,
with enthusiasm anew.

I've returned to the Enchanted Mountains,
on many occasions since then,
but not even once did I feel the urge to climb on their rock again,
I'm content to gaze in wonder, for it's a bit like coming home,
as I say hello to my silent friends; those shepherds
now turned to stone.

40: Adagio without strings

Night-time retains its quota of stars
and the moon still clings to the sky,
while down in the valley beside my tent
a frozen stream slides by.
Stiff I am and aching
as I crawl out to start the day.
My eyes still burn from lack of sleep,
my tongue is as thick as clay.
But ahead stretch hours of activity
among snowfields and glaciers and rocks,
a day I'll survive, if I'm lucky,
with no thought for time marked by clocks.

A couple of hours, I guess it is,
when there comes the first hint of dawn,
as light stretches over the mountains
to tell me a new day's been born.
I watch the sun rise out in the east
and face its welcome glow,
then step upon the glacier
still dusted with yesterday's snow.
The icefield goes on for ever
striped with crevasses here and there,
warnings, if any were needed,
that each one be treated with care.

As the day wears on and the sun climbs high,
I trade that icefield for snow,
and then a ragged crown of rocks
suggests which way I should go.
A final ridge gives a walk in thin air
and the summit at last is won.
I stretch my arms up to the sky
and try to reach the sun.
Turning in a circle I gather in the view
that bears no hint of mankind's touch,
but is as though the world is new.

My descent is slow, I must admit,
it's been a long and demanding climb.
My toes are sore, fingers torn,
I have no idea of time.
My nose is cracked and blistered,
but I couldn't care one jot
though I know when I reach the valley
all my energy will be shot.
I swear that none of this matters
I've had a day I'll never forget,
and I'll relive each joyful moment
when at last I watch the sun set.

Best of all is this evening time
when I relax beside the stream
with the mountains gathered all around
reminding me where I've been.

The little stove hissing beside me
says a meal is on its way,
something that will sustain me
for another climbing day.
Twilight is when the valley is calm,
it's when Nature softly sings.
It's the long day's final adagio
an adagio without strings.

41: The memory box

There's a big storage box in my garage
with a record of most of my schemes.
Sometimes I go there to forage
and disturb a lifetime of dreams.
The journals in which they're recorded
are stacked in batches of ten,
and ever since they were sorted
I've had reason to sort them again.
All of the journals have covers,
most are red but some faded blue
to distinguish one set from the others,
or they did once, when they were new.

The first one I usually reach for
dates from the summer of 'sixty-five
when I dared to stray outside my door
and suddenly came alive.
T'was the year of my first expedition
to mountains a long way from home,
a lifestyle turned into obsession
as I sought more wild places to roam.
Out there the high Atlas Mountains
turned my life all around
for I saw that just like fountains
salvation was there to be found.

So I ditched my work in an office block
and escaped to the Alps in the snow,
where I never bothered to look at the clock
or questioned when I should go.
From Switzerland I then worked in Austria,
then back to the Swiss I adore,
expenses may have been costlier,
but my earnings were so much more.
But I've never cared about money
while there's sufficient to pay the bills
for there's a land of milk and honey
to be found among the hills.

I fell in love with the Pyrenees,
they became my spiritual home.
In twenty-four hours I could be there with ease,
with family, friends or alone.
My journals tell of countless hills
I visited for my books,
days 'out there' could cure any ills
on each expedition I took.
Many remind me of treks in Nepal,
some of Bhutan and Ladakh,
but one thing they share in common with all
is the whisper that lures me back.

When Russia was still in the USSR
I stood on the Caucasus heights,
always aware not to stray too far

being watched through the day and the night.
There's a journal that tells of the Andes,
those mountains of Peru,
where someone warned me of bandits,
but my guide saw me safely through.
There's another from eastern Turkey,
and climbing Mount Ararat.
While some were sick I felt perky
before descending to Dogubayazat

From Norway's broad-backed ridges
to its deep sheer-sided fjords
I was reminded of glacial fridges
where today the waterfalls roared.
Sent to the Tatras of Poland
I stayed in a guesthouse below,
approached through a patchwork of lowland
with plenty of rain but no snow.
At the far eastern end of the Alpine chain
I explored Slovenia's heights,
then found an excuse to go back again
to bivouac on warm summer nights.

Speaking of heights, the Dolomites
burst out of pastures green.
They really are an incredible sight,
the most exotic peaks that I've seen.
Each page of the journals I study
brings alive the sounds and the smells,

the stain of fingers once bloodied
recall many times that I fell.
Most entries I wrote at the end of the day
whilst curled up in my tent,
and the wind would try to sweep it away
leaving all the poles badly bent.

Time may have faded a lot of the ink,
some pages are grubby and curled,
but I only need a moment to think
of great days in the mountain world.
So I go to my box in the garage
and wonder, where shall I travel today,
where's the best place to forage
and there I'll happily stray.
Yes, life can be full of wonder,
there's adventure and beauty galore
if you're brave enough to plunder
the world outside your door.

42: Sleeping around

I spent the nights in a wide range of beds
in the years I was travelling around,
some had pillows, a few had sheets,
a number were flat on the ground.

I dossed under and on top of tables,
one in a signalman's shed,
and was woken in time for breakfast
so the signalman could be fed.

One time an old tented hostel
on an island of sand dunes and pines
was hit by a massive storm one night
and I was bombed by cones several times.

I swung in a hammock on an ex-army truck
driving south through sun-baked Spain.
Most of the time I felt seasick,
but I'd do it all over again.

Wand'ring through deep Atlas valleys,
looking for somewhere to sleep, I was shown
that in every village I came to
there's a flat roof on each Berber's home.

The summer I worked in Austria
I ferried my groups there and back,

travelling on Europe's fine railways,
stretched out on the luggage rack.

The floor of numerous stations
bear the imprint of my head,
while the cushions of airport lounges
create the most comfortable bed.

I dozed on many a mountain peak
under duvets consisting of stars,
but the worst of all the nights I spent
were on the back seats of moving cars.

There was a freezing night in a Sherpa's lodge
surrounded by ice and snow,
where the thermometer dropped in our bedroom
to a grim sixteen below.

I've kipped in countless meadows
not always in a tent
aware of the songs of a babbling brook
that lulled me to sleep content.

I was flooded out of my tent one night
in the Écrins National Park
I grabbed my passport and rucksack
and fled to safety in the dark.

I slept on a bed of nettles,
they smelled good but boy did they sting,

I tell you I'll not do that again
so at least I did learn something.

Mountain huts were some of the best
so far from the nearest town,
the only thing I regretted
were snorers with their own surround sound.

In an unmanned hut one springtime
the snow began to thaw,
when in the night an avalanche
covered the roof and blocked the door.

I've dossed in some dodgy dwellings
from Paris to old Kathmandu,
some of them had no bathroom,
just a truly revolting loo.

There's been geckos climbing the bedroom walls,
mice scampering all over the floor.
I've slept with my money belt under my head
when my host had no care for the law.

I've slept with one eye wide open,
a chair or two blocking the door,
I've even woken shaking with fear
when I heard a strange creature roar.

But of all the nights I spent away,
there were few that filled me with dread.
Only now I'd much rather be at home
with my wife in our soft double bed.

43: Helga

Helga! Yes Helga,
that could have been her name,
a bronze-limbed, wild-eyed lioness
with a lion's regal mane.
Fit, she was, and raunchy,
with teeth as white as pearls,
a German lass from Düsseldorf
the pick of all the girls.

I saw her first in Langtang
when trekking with some friends,
alone with just a Sherpa
to carry odds and ends.
She appeared from out of nowhere
like a comet in the night,
after ten hours on the go that day
she still looked fresh and bright.

She pitched her tent quite close to mine
in pastures grazed by yaks
(those sharp-horned stubborn beasties
with hairy coats upon their backs).
A vision of raw beauty
was my neighbour for the night.
I lay awake for hours
looking forward to the light.

The next day she had gone
before my tent was down and dry,
the well-bronzed German bombshell
heading where the eagles fly.
And next time that I saw her
in a street in Kathmandu
she smiled and gave a Namaste
and whispered 'how are you?'

A year went by and I went back
for trekking in Nepal,
and camped one night in clear view's sight
of the Khumbu's great ice-fall,
when I heard a voice I recognised
with its earthy German tone.
And there was bronze-limbed Helga
setting up her tented home.

The summer next in Grindelwald
above all mountain streams
around the bend strode Helga
like a vision from my dreams.
She threw her arms around me
and kissed me on the cheek,
my friend who was walking with me, said
'you'll wash no more this week.'

Oh Helga! Yes, my Helga
was playing with my heart

for she broke it for a third time
when she said 'now we must part.'
We watched her storming down the trail
'til she'd disappeared from view
when my friend asked me mischievously
'how does she know you?'

Two more times I saw her
on Himalayan trails,
as a consequence of all of that
she was the subject of wild tales.
But now my days of trekking
are just memories from the past
while Helga, yes bronze Helga
still makes my heart beat fast.

Now before you get the wrong idea,
there's something I'll explain.
The way that she and I would meet
time and time again
was nothing but coincidence;
strange – but this is true,
I wouldn't try to pull your leg
or tell a lie to you.
We had no sly encounter
no Himalayan tryst
but mountains without Helga
are like mountains hid by mist.

44: The old man of the mountains

For weeks I wandered all alone across the Himalaya,
from passes high I'd count the ranges layer after layer.
Mountains scratching heaven's blue,
rock and ice and snowfields too
they filled my eyes with every view
and graced each hour with wonder.

One day when sun glanced off the snow
I saw some tracks that seemed to go
to places where the cold winds blow
far from any gompa.
No prayer flags there, no sign of man,
I thought then I would make a plan
to treat this pristine mountain land
just like a Shangri La.

Shangri La, now that's a thought,
I wondered if I really ought
to see what those strange tracks had brought
me out here to discover.
I kept each one within my sight,
followed them both day and night.
While frosted in the pale moonlight
they always made me shiver.

At last they topped a long steep hill,
it seemed as if all life stood still
for there I sensed a joyful thrill
that set my heart a-quiver.
With no more snow I looked below
to see a rich green meadow,
snd there lit by a campfire glow
a man stood by a river.

He was no ordinary man,
at least not from a distant scan.
Up to the moon his deep voice sang
a song just like no other.
But then – I know this seems absurd –
I understood each tuneful word,
its message like a mournful bird
calling for a lover.

'Come down' it said 'and join me here,
you really have no need to fear,
this extraordinary year
is one you will remember.
The reason that you chose to roam
so far from all you feared at home,
down here that virus is unknown,
for sickness is a stranger.'

What land was this that I had found?
It felt somehow like sacred ground,

a place where I was surely bound
to find what I'd been seeking.
Seeking what? You may well ask,
I felt that I'd been set a task
to learn how long the bug would last
and would it keep repeating.

I looked the stranger in the eye,
his mouth fell open, made a sigh
that sounded like a joyful cry
as if he'd found a brother.
He had no clothes, his stubby nose
wobbled just like blubber,
he wore a frown, his arms hung down,
his knees rubbed one another.

'The answer to your quest is clear, but you must try to be sincere
or you will never learn it.
Sow a seed that ends all greed –
then perhaps you'll earn it,
but treat the Earth as though it's worth
no more than you take from it,
it will fight back and you will lack
the wherewithal to stop it.'

I thought about his sage advice
and looked at what seemed Paradise.
There's wisdom in his words I thought,
something good that can't be bought.

I pondered on them, long and deep,
then lay down and fell asleep.
In dreams a voice said 'You've no choice,
but please do not forget me'
and when I woke I saw who spoke
was no-one but a yeti.

45: Sacred ground

High in the Himalaya, north-east of Kathmandu,
there's a modest-looking mountain
with an extraordinary view.
I've stood upon its summit three times that I recall,
and reckon what you see from there's
the finest view of all.

I first trekked the Solu Khumbu when researching for a book.
I'd heard so much about it
that I thought I'd have a look.
I'd already witnessed wonders, but this to my surprise
left me truly breathless
as the tears sprang from my eyes.

I returned some six years later in the company of my wife
who confessed the whole experience
was the highlight of her life.
We had a Sherpa with us then, Krishna was his name,
who nodded in agreement
and said he felt the same.

There was snow on that occasion, it pained our searching eyes
while far below we heard the sounds
of Tibetan snow-cocks' cries.
The day was filled with beauty, we hardly spoke at all
but let the mountains speak for us,
then responded to their call.

One year I took a group of friends who came from far and wide
whose delight at what they saw that day
was impossible to hide.
The prayer flags on the summit fluttered in a breeze
to calm their cries of wonder
and put everyone at ease.

So what's its name and where's it found, this mountain with a view?
And how can we approach it
if we start in Kathmandu?
Well, you can trek for several weeks, or you can fly there on a plane.
I guess it doesn't matter
for the views will be the same.

I much prefer to trek there from the foothills in the west
and sleep in village houses
with the folk I love the best.
But if you fly to Lukla you will have some extra days
to spend in Solu Khumbu
to acclimatise and gaze.

Just around the corner from Namche's bustling town
there's a valley flanked by mountains
whose glaciers cascade down.
Pushing through the valley there's the wildest of them all,
it's called the Ngozumpa,
the longest in Nepal.

You'll trek beside this glacier to a string of turquoise lakes
in a rough ablation valley
among moraine the glacier makes.
At last a group of lodges is seen huddled in the snow,
its name, as is the hill above,
is simply Gokyo.

The hill's a minor mountain, though five thousand metres high
and under good conditions
needs more breath than skill to try.
But once you reach the very top and stand upon its crown
you'll imagine you're in heaven
for there's glory all around.

Eight thousand metre mountains dominate the view:
Makalu and Everest,
Lhotse, Cho Oyu.
But everywhere you rest your eyes the view is so serene
it's not so much reality
as a figment of a dream.

So there we are, the secret's out, you'll know now where to go,
off to the Himalaya
to trek to Gokyo.
And if by chance you reach the top, try not to make a sound
for truth be told this rocky crown
is God's own sacred ground.

46: Kangchenjunga dreaming

I was dreaming of Kangchenjunga last night.
Yes I know it's a long way away,
but it's off to the high Himalaya
that my thoughts will sometimes stray.
It's not that I am discontented –
please don't get me wrong,
but lockdown plays havoc with the best of minds,
and mine never was that strong.
So forgive this little diversion
from the mundane of much of my day
and come with me on a journey or two
where the yeti is said to play.

Now sunrise on Kangchenjunga
is one of the World's great sights,
especially when you've been tucked in a tent
on a cold and frosty night.
The very first time that I saw it
was thirty long years ago.
It was two weeks' walk from the foothills,
an enormous fortress of snow,
that seemed to float on a far-off cloud
tinged with the rising sun.
My Sherpa friends were speechless,
enriched by the prize they'd won.

Long before we could reach it
our trail was a terrible tease.
Our foreheads would drip in the daytime,
while at nighttime our water would freeze.
We trekked through steamy jungles
beneath white-faced monkeys at play,
and stopped at wayside gompas
so our Sherpa sirdar could pray.
And every step of every day
was like the notes of a much-loved song
that rang in my ears to banish all fears:
'This is where you belong.'

Two weeks on and we stood at its base,
more than four thousand metres or so,
as the dawn escaped from Sikkim's grip
to make all the mountains glow.
I stood there beside my two Sherpa friends,
Pemba and Dendi their names.
Softly spoken Buddhists,
in the abode of the gods so they claimed.
'Now pray like we do,' they urged me,
'that one day you'll come back once more,'
So I did, and I'm happy to tell you,
I've been there not one time, but four.

I've made journeys to its South Face,
and trekked to its far North-West.
I once led a group on the frontier ridge,

but couldn't say which was the best.
This massif with five mighty summits,
one the third highest on Earth
defies any crude estimation
of what its scenic value is worth.
Back in the nineteenth century
it was admired by men of the Raj
when furloughed up in Darjeeling
where the British were firmly in charge.

I've captured that sunrise from Darjeeling's hills,
and floundered on Sikkim's wet trails,
and three times seduced by the ways of Nepal
whose romance never fails.
The hill folk in their villages,
their terraced fields in the sun
direct the way to the land of the gods
where egos are often undone.
I'll never go back there, I know it,
but I tell you I have no regret
for the adventures of my younger days
are impossible to forget.

47: Journey to Ladakh

It was four days to Leh from Manali
on a road not much more than a track.
Four days over challenging passes
to that high mountain desert, Ladakh.
Four days with a squint-eyed driver
in a car with four dodgy tyres,
But I admit I loved every moment,
for adventure is what life requires.

There were monsoon rains in Manali,
the mountains covered with clouds,
The main street was all but deserted,
only the monkeys gathered in crowds.
The Rhotang La was closed, they said,
thanks to a major mud slide,
but our driver was deaf to such warnings
and pushed the barriers aside.

Manic and bloody-minded
he pressed his foot hard down on the floor,
while my friends and I behind him
knew what the seat belts were for.
The road twisted out of the valley
towards that first high threatening pass,
with our driver staring intently
through the mud-stained windscreen glass.

Yet we made it to the Rhotang La,
though I couldn't tell you how,
and whooped with exhilaration
for the rain clouds were clearing now.
We descended in shafts of sunlight
to Lahoul where I once longed to stray
while glad our first pass was over
and that we'd live for another day.

That night we camped by a gompa –
a monastery still being built.
It overlooked a river
that curled between wide banks of silt.
Dog roses brightened the flanks
of the high Himalayan hills
and prayer flags fluttered above us,
bringing protection from all of life's ills.

A day or two later we reached the top
of the bleak Baralacha La,
a vast open windswept plateau
on a track not made for a car.
We rested there an hour or more,
in a landscape out of my dreams,
gazing into tomorrow,
or that is how it now seems.

Out of the hills came a dust cloud
kicked up by a huge flock of sheep.

led by a voiceless shepherd
who walked as though half asleep.
The sheep looked neither right nor left,
and became a part of our view,
continuing in a dead-straight line
'til they'd vanished into the blue.

Where had they come from and where did they go
in that vast land of nothing where only winds blow?
Nothing to graze on and no running stream,
nothing to say where the shepherd had been.
It was almost a mirage, it didn't seem real,
I was curious, bewildered, unsure how to feel.
I'd stood on the summit, gazed out into space
when they came, and they went, not leaving a trace.

When daylight slid behind the hills
and shadows gathered round
we spent the night in two-man tents
pegged tight against the ground.
Marmots hid in burrows,
flowers made stars in the grass,
it was all so very different
from the Baralacha Pass.

On and on our journey went
through country harsh, untamed.
Mountains and deep canyons
and more passes without names.

Our squint-eyed driver laughing still
just like a man possessed,
a man of boundless energy
who seemed to need no rest.

And then we topped our final pass,
one of the highest in the world
where at 5441 metres
tattered prayer flags were unfurled.
It was there our manic driver
found a puncture in one tyre
and replaced it with another
whose condition was just as dire.

Looking down upon our winding road
with scores of hairpin bends
I wondered if we'd make it,
or could this be the end?
Way down there in the distance
I saw a river's gleam
and guessed it was the Indus,
the answer to my dream.

The Indus flowing through Ladakh
to the wilds of Pakistan,
between two mountain ranges,
the highest known to man.
Ladakh – that hidden desert land
bordered by Tibet

had trapped me with its romance
like a fish caught in a net.

And here we were three hours from Leh,
so near and yet so far.
Three hours is less than half a day,
if you've a guardian star.
But who knows if we'd last three hours
to safely make it there?
Not much chance of that, I thought,
since our driver seems not to care.

But down we went at breakneck speed,
old squint-eye laughing loud,
scraping round each corner
to the car horn's warning sound.
Then we crossed the Indus
just an hour outside of Leh
where our suicidal driver
had once more saved the day.

The ancient cracked-wall capital
of mystical Ladakh,
Leh looked across the Indus plain
to mountains standing back.
An ever-changing landscape
three thousand metres high
whose snow peaks in the distance
scratched the Himalayan sky.

The Indus spawned oases
with groups of fruiting trees,
while the sound of chanting lamas
was carried by the breeze.
Old gompas clung to awesome cliffs
whichever way you'd look
reminding me of Shangri-La,
our modern world forsook.

So, thanks to squint-eye's driving
we were lucky to survive
and in this hidden paradise
were glad to be alive.
Though we'd spend the next few weeks
exploring old Ladakh
I knew the moment I arrived
that I'd be coming back.

48: A time and a place to remember

A weary descent from the mountains,
four days from the snow and the ice
brought us to the foothills
with their terraces of rice.
The crops were ready for harvesting,
dried by the summer's sun
so farmers with sharp-edged sickles
were at work soon as day had begun.

It was hot down there, my word it was hot,
our shirts were drenched with sweat,
I yearned to be back in the mountains again,
as high as I could get.
But through stinging eyes when not bothered by flies
I could see the foothills' charms
where surrounded by so much activity
were clusters of straw-thatched farms.

Bananas grew all around them,
marigolds hung from their eaves,
buffalo shook their dusty-black heads
while seeking shade among trees,
goats and their kids looked for something to graze,
and cocks would constantly crow
while we scratched our heads in bewilderment,
unsure of the way we should go.

There was nothing to tell us where we were,
or where we were going to,
and the crumpled map in my sweaty hand
offered no sign of a clue.
An old man squatting at his door
looked up with quizzical eyes,
and I'd say by his demeanour
his great age had made him wise.

My Sherpa friend strolled over to him
and gave him a warm Namaste,
then after a short conversation
asked if he could possibly tell us the way.
He had several teeth missing, this wizened old man,
but that didn't detract from his smile,
when he patted the ground beside him and said:
'Why not sit here for a while?'

'There's no need to be in a hurry,' he said,
'in a few hours the sun will go down.
Maybe you'd like to camp for the night,
I own a spare patch of ground.'
My Sherpa friend wiped the sweat from his neck
and thought that his plan was just fine,
after struggling all day through that tropical heat
he was glad we now had some time.

The tents went up on a stubbly patch
where rice had previously grown.

To reach it we'd squeeze through a large stand of trees
not far from the old man's home.
At last the sun went down in the west
and I detected a welcoming breeze,
that carried the foothills' scents and sounds
amid the rustling of the leaves.

We were visited by some children
once our meal was over and done.
Then came their parents and old village folk,
smiling, every one.
They hung garlands of flowers around our necks,
pressed a bindi on each cooling brow,
then sat on the ground before us,
while I wondered - what happens now?

I was blessed I guess by that gesture,
as I know my friends were too,
for Pemba now lit a Tilly lamp
so we could see just who was who.
A young man then got up on his feet
and gave a welcoming speech,
how happy his neighbours were, he said,
that we chose to stay within reach.

Another young man tap-tapped on a drum,
two more of them burst into song
while all the girls stood up to dance,
their shyness by now had gone.

They raised their arms high into the air,
bare feet kept faith with the tune,
then one by one we joined them to dance
in the light of the rising moon.

That evening was one of pure magic,
full of wonders we could never expect,
the dancing, the singing, the warmth of the welcome,
we wondered - what's coming next?
A basket of fresh bananas appeared,
they were handed to one and all
while far away in the distance
I could hear the night birds call.

We'd be up and away next morning
before the heat of the day grew intense,
so thanking the good folk their friendship
we drifted off to our tents.
But I hardly slept a wink that night,
if I did it was only to dream
of the old man's invitation to stay
that was better than at first it had seemed.

Mist hung over the harvest fields,
the mountains were hidden from view
as we collapsed our heavy dew-damp tents
to begin the day anew.
We'd planned to creep away
and not disturb our new-found friends

but they were already waiting
at the point where their village ends.

The smiling women stood in line
dressed in their brightest clothes
to bless us on our journey
with that familiar Namaste pose.
With garlands still around our necks,
fresh flowers were placed in our hair
and to top it all
the scent of frangipani hung in the air.

The spokesman from the night before
then kindly pointed the way
but told us that before we left
there was something he'd like to say.
'You're among the first to come here,
and last night was our happiest yet
so I hope you will remember us,' he said,
'please try not to forget.'

I shook him warmly by the hand,
and wiped away a tear
and wondered if I'd find the way back
if I came another year.
For no map showed the village,
it was as though it didn't exist
and when I turned to wave farewell,
it had vanished in the mist.

I've said it once, I've said it twice,
and I'll say it one more time,
the most rewarding days of a mountain trip
are not found on the peaks you climb.

49: In the saddle

I doubt you'll have heard of Mugu,
it's in a hidden part of Nepal.
As few outsiders had been there before,
I couldn't resist its call.
The trouble with that is I hadn't been back
to the Himalaya for years,
for TB or not, my lungs were both shot,
though I harboured no other fears.
So I called my very good Sherpa friend
and asked him what we should do.
He said: 'Let's take an expedition,
and I'll organise a crew.'
That left me the problem of crossing each pass.
My Sherpa friend said 'Of course
I have the perfect solution for you,
I'll arrange to get you a horse.'

I hadn't been in a saddle
since donkey rides on a beach.
If anything happened in Mugu,
any help would be way out of reach,
Yet that unknown land haunted my dreams,
so I said okay let's go,
I'll face any problems that come my way
and learn all there is to know.
We flew as far as Jumla,
a foothill township that we knew

where my expedition friends and I
met the pony men and the crew.
Sangye the horse was set for the course,
though she looked ungainly not sleek,
yet I soon discovered the best of mounts
is the one with four steady feet.

After three full days we set up our tents
on the shores of Rara Lake,
where jackals howled throughout the night –
what a blood-curdling sound they make!
But when we continued the following day,
with the sun climbing out of Tibet,
the snow peaks on the horizon
gave the most beautiful views as yet.
Beyond the lake the way would make
us weave through a stand of pine,
and there we came to a vantage point
looking down on a steep incline.
We could see where we were heading,
it was a wild and lonely glen,
a country full of mystery,
it was a privilege to share it with friends.

Oh the thrill that comes with the call of the wild,
it creates the most joyful of days
when you perch on the lip of a steep plunging cliff,
and simply stand and gaze.
But I was sitting on Sangye

who's head was bothered by flies,
so we set off down a twisting trail
to the sound of the pony men's cries.
On the hillsides to the right of us
were piles of harvested grain,
and when we turned a prominent spur,
found the left-hand side the same.
As we wandered through Gamghadi
the villagers crowded around.
It must have looked to them as if
the circus had come to town.

At the foot of a series of ragged hills
we plunged into a gorge,
a valley full of twists and turns
where a rocky trail had been forged.
The days were full of ups and downs,
the nights were crisp and cold,
and with every hour on Sangye's back
the more I was feeling bold.
She and I were friends by now,
she'd whinny when I came near
knowing I guess, though a bit of a mess,
I no longer had any fear.
Until one day on a near-vertical rock
I felt the saddle slide
and fell like a sack from poor Sangye's back,
but the gods were all on my side.

So close were we to the mountains
we couldn't see their peaks,
but their flanks were fearfully rugged
to ensure their secrets would keep.
The river roared through tight ravines,
it was always on our right,
except on rare occasions
when we'd cross to camp for the night.
Pack ponies carried our supplies,
attended by three men,
plus a cook and two of his helpers,
and of course my good Sherpa friend.
As deeper we went through that magical land,
not knowing what to expect
I came to admire my four-legged friend
with more and more respect.

At last the valley broke in two,
both rivers flashed and foamed.
My Sherpa friend said head to the north
and we'll come to an old Buddhist home.
A rough trail took us higher,
with tiny meadows here and there
on which we'd set our tents at night,
with not much room to spare.
Then one November morning
as the night clouds swept away,
I was so pleased when on the breeze
I heard some Buddhists pray.

That sound drew us steadily closer,
one cautious step at a time
until we spied a village
at the top of a steep incline.

A cluster of flat-roofed houses
were gathered three sides of a square,
in the centre of which stood a gompa,
alive with the mumbling of prayer.
A monk in a tattered old tunic
beckoned us inside the door,
where my Sherpa and the pony men too
prostrated themselves on the floor.
Once their devotions were over
the monk led us back to his home,
a smoke-blackened one-roomed hermit's house
in which he lived all alone.
We sat on the roof in the midday sun,
blessed by the old man's grace
as he offered a bowl of potatoes
with a smile upon his face.

No less than three lammergeier
with wing span a full nine feet
sailed the thermals around us,
'til we could almost touch each beak.
The ruffling of their feathers,
the steely look in their eyes
add to the wonders of this day

that was now so full of surprise.
Tibet we were told was an hour away,
but we had no right to go there.
Besides there's nowhere I wanted to be
but on that roof overlooking the square.
The best of days are the simple days,
expect little and you'll gain so much
as with the monk on that Mugu roof,
and lammergeier we'd almost touch.

A series of unnamed passes
had to be crossed when our way turned for home,
Each one four thousand metres or more
linked by ridges on which we would roam.
My friends were strung out behind me,
plus the pony men and the crew,
while I raised myself from the saddle
in an attempt to absorb the view.
That view stretched out for ever
as we journeyed it seemed in the sky
far from habitation, up there where the eagles fly.
The horizon was streaked by a line of snow peaks
with shadows in between
as our journey took us to places
where few others had ever been.

Yes, I thought I'd gone to heaven
as on Sangye's back I rode
while my Sherpa friend and the others
were speechless as they strode.

But when at last we crossed the last pass
and descended into a glen,
the crew set to and made a fine camp,
for us and the pony men.
And there we stayed for two memorable days
where the autumn flowers were bright,
and the moon came up with a million stars
to fill the sky each night.
I didn't need to be told I was now too old
to see these mountains again,
when I said farewell to Mugu,
while ruffling my horse's mane.

At home on my computer
I have a thousand photos or more.
But none of these recalls the thrill
of the wilderness we saw.
And the notes I made in my journal
only hint at adventures gained,
while the mysterious monk and his gompa
have yet to be explained.
The roar of a river through a gorge,
the sound of a jackal's cry,
the seething of insects in the sun
as we slowly wandered by.
Though tough at times and demanding,
there's nothing to detract
from the joy of riding in the sky
on dear old Sangye's back.

50: The hidden land

We sit upon our final pass, my Sherpa friend and I,
the mountains fading blue towards the west.
Our journey through the Hidden Land is one I won't deny
will count among the toughest and the best.

The Hidden Land is simply that; some fear its desolation
but at its very heart we found a long lost population.
They live a hard but simple life, in a medieval world,
their communities protected by the prayer flags they've unfurled.

They have no need of highways, their roads are unmarked tracks
created by the journeys made by heavy-laden yaks.
They have no schools, no health posts, no radio or tv
but I somehow gained the impression they were
more content than me.

The Hidden Land's protected by the Himalayan range,
its valleys higher than so many peaks;
the landscape's oh so different, and some even think it strange
that to cross from east to west takes several weeks.

We trekked through ice-carved gorges where the sun
would never shine,
we turned our backs on trees and shrubs and flowers,
we scrambled over passes to see what we would find
and breathed the air of freedom through the hours.

Old gompas on the hillsides where Buddhas gather dust
    were built at least five hundred years ago.
That's when a few brave traders broke the barren untouched crust
    to find some soil in which their crops could grow.

In tiny groups of houses standing several hours apart
    we sat and drank their salted butter tea.
The smoke from yak-dung fires filled our lungs right from the start
    until coughing helped us gain our liberty.

There were no maps to show the way,
    no weather-beaten cairns of local stone,
instead we found a shepherd late one cold autumnal day
    and a wizened wild-eyed trader far from home.

They pointed out the route they said would lead from here to there,
    so up we trudged through slips of icy snow
that took us to a ridge-top where the wind had stripped it bare
    to reveal a maze of valleys far below.

Day after day, week after week, we trekked this Hidden Land
    whose scenes of savage grandeur were a feast,
each glacier pass, each walled moraine would make its own demand,
    each hour would see our mutual joy increase.

But now we've reached our final pass, my Sherpa friend and I,
    he tells me there are just three days to go.
Yet far off in our western view, and floating in the sky
    appears what seems a mighty peak of snow.

'What's that?' I ask, 'that block of snow which dominates our view?
I'd like to know its valleys and its peaks.'
He screws his eyes and makes a grin, then says 'Just me and you
must go there, but we'll need a good few weeks.'
And so another plan is born, that's how my life has been,
with every new day's promised dawn,
another tempting dream.

Printed in Great Britain
by Amazon